FAR EAST VS. WILD WEST

Skye Fargo had seen what the strange art of karate could do when the earl chopped down a huge Indian brave and killed him as easily as snapping a twig.

Now it was Fargo's turn. He did not even see the earl's kick coming. His vision swam and his knees buckled. Through sheer force of will he stayed upright.

Anger made Fargo step forward and punch. He should have known better. A moment later he was flying head over heels, tumbling in the dust. Bruised and aching, he heard mocking laughter.

"You don't stand a chance, and you're too stupid to realize it," the earl said. "I was taught by the master Kano himself."

The earl smiled then as he advanced toward Fargo. "I want to relish this. I want to whittle you down piece by piece and hear your screams when I break you apart."

The earl was a human killing machine, and all the Trailsman had were kicks as fast as lightning and hands as deadly as twin axes.

THE TRAILSMAN #152
PRAIRIE FIRE

THE TRAILSMAN
152

PRAIRIE FIRE

by

Jon Sharpe

A SIGNET BOOK

SIGNET

Published by the Penguin Group
Penguin Books USA Inc., 375 Hudson Street,
New York, New York 10014, U.S.A.
Penguin Books Ltd, 27 Wrights Lane,
London W8 5TZ, England
Penguin Books Australia Ltd, Ringwood,
Victoria, Australia
Penguin Books Canada Ltd, 10 Alcorn Avenue,
Toronto, Ontario, Canada M4V 3B2
Penguin Books (N.Z.) Ltd, 182–190 Wairau Road,
Auckland 10, New Zealand

Penguin Books Ltd, Registered Offices:
Harmondsworth, Middlesex, England

First published by Signet,
an imprint of Dutton Signet,
a division of Penguin Books USA Inc.

First Printing, August, 1994
10 9 8 7 6 5 4 3 2 1

The first chapter of this book previously appeared in *Crowheart's Revenge*, the one
hundred and fifty-first volume in this series.

 REGISTERED TRADEMARK—MARCA REGISTRADA

Printed in the United States of America

The Trailsman

Beginnings . . . they bend the tree and they mark the man. Skye Fargo was born when he was eighteen. Terror was his midwife, vengeance his first cry. Killing spawned Skye Fargo, ruthless, cold-blooded murder. Out of the acrid smoke of gunpowder still hanging in the air, he rose, cried out a promise never forgotten.

The Trailsman they began to call him all across the West: searcher, scout, hunter, the man who could see where others only looked, his skills for hire but not his soul, the man who lived each day to the fullest, yet trailed each tomorrow. Skye Fargo, the Trailsman, and the seeker who could take the wildness of a land and the wanting of a woman and make them his own.

1860, the vast Plains—
where savage men
and savage beasts
made life a living hell . . .

1

The last thing a man expects to hear when he is in the middle of a vast plain, surrounded on all sides by a sea of shimmering grass, is the merry tinkle of female laughter. Yet that is exactly what Skye Fargo heard as he rode slowly westward, and the instant he did he reined up and looked around. The sound had faded and Fargo wondered if his ears were playing tricks on him. Then it was repeated.

Puzzled, the big man guided his pinto stallion to the northwest, in the direction of the mirth. The presence of a woman was a mystery he couldn't ignore, especially since he was so far off the beaten track it was doubtful any other whites had ever visited the region before, except maybe for a few buffalo hunters.

Indians were another matter. Both the Sioux and the Cheyenne hunted buffalo there regularly. Occasionally the Arapaho did the same. But they never brought their women along, so far as Fargo knew.

A gap in the waving grass appeared, a break that told Fargo there was a gully ahead. Stopping, he ground-hitched the Ovaro and shucked his Sharps from its saddle scabbard, then inserted a cartridge and warily advanced. He had no idea what he would run into, but it never paid to take anything for granted when out in the wild.

The breeze carried voices to Fargo's ears. A man spoke first, a woman answered.

"—finally alone, I have something I want to say."

"Don't spoil it, Jeems."

"You know how much I want you, Flora. You're on my mind every bleeding minute of the day, from the time I wake up until I fall asleep."

"Did you hear yourself?" the woman responded testily.

"You *want* me. You don't love me. I doubt you even care for me all that much. All I am is convenient."

"Don't be like this. Here, luv. Give us a kiss."

There was a rustling noise, followed by a loud slap. Fargo came to the rim of the gully and hunkered down in the high grass to see what was going on. The clipped accents of the speakers had added to his perplexity, but they in no way prepared him for the surprise he felt on seeing the struggling pair below.

A pert redhead, whose long hair was up in a bun, was fighting off the amorous advances of a stocky man sporting a thin mustache and a neatly trimmed goatee. It wasn't the style of their hair that was so surprising, but rather the way in which they were dressed.

The woman had on a uniform of some sort, consisting of a starched white blouse with frills at the front and a knee-length black skirt that flared at the bottom. She also wore black hose and, of all things, dainty shoes with incredibly high heels.

Not to be outdone, the man had on a fancy three-piece black suit and shoes of the same color, which were polished so highly they gleamed in the sunlight. A white shirt and black cravat completed his wardrobe.

Fargo could scarcely credit his own eyes. Here he was, in the middle of the vast prairie, in the heart of Indian country, and he'd stumbled on two fools dressed in their Sunday go-to-meeting clothes. He didn't know what to make of it, but he did know how to react to the plight the woman faced. Standing, he stepped to the edge of the slope, trained the Sharps on Fancy Suit, and said matter-of-factly, "I'd get off the lady right quick, mister, unless you're partial to the idea of having your backside blown clean off."

At the first syllable the man glanced up, turned beet-red, and jumped to his feet. He seemed about to say something, until he realized the Sharps was trained on his midsection.

The woman rose slowly, brushing grass and dirt from her skirt. She cocked her pretty head and regarded Fargo quizzically. "You don't look like the knight-in-shining-armor type, but I reckon a girl has to make do in a pinch." Her red lips curled upward. "Flora Livingstone, at your service big man."

"Skye Fargo."

"Do you live hereabouts?"

Fargo had to laugh. "Lady, do you have any damn idea where the hell you are?"

Her smile broadened. "If you ask me, I'm in hell. Although I'm a bit put out that they got it all wrong. Instead of fire and brimstone, there's nothing but this bloody grass."

Keeping the rifle fixed on the livid man, Fargo walked to the bottom of the gully and openly admired the redheaded woman's curvaceous figure. "From where I'm standing, it looks as if I've found me a slice of heaven on earth."

Flora chuckled, her green eyes narrowing. "Aren't you the brazen one. I don't know whether to be flattered or upset. Could it be I've gone from the frying pan into the fire?"

"I don't force myself on women," Fargo said sternly.

She pursed her mouth a moment. "No, I don't suppose you would have to. I bet a handsome man like you has to fight the ladies off with a broom." Her attention strayed to her companion. "You're lucky this gentleman came along when he did, Jeems. If you'd persisted, I would have seen fit to tell the earl."

"You bloody bitch—" Jeems growled, but got no further.

Skye Fargo took a single stride and rammed the stock of his rifle into the man's stomach. Jeems doubled over, sputtering, and stumbled to one side. A second blow, delivered to his temple, felled him in his tracks.

"My word!" Flora declared. "Did you have to do that?"

"He needs to learn some manners," Fargo said, and was flabbergasted when she threw back her head and brayed like a mule. "What did I say?"

"Manners are what Jeems is all about." Flora adjusted her blouse and gave the unconscious man a nudge with her toe. "He's one of the earl's two manservants."

"Who is this earl you keep talking about?"

"Perhaps you'd like to meet him? You can escort us back to camp."

"I'll escort you," Fargo corrected her. "Your friend can lie there and rot, for all I care."

"Outspoken soul, aren't you?"

"I don't believe in beating around the bush, if that's what you mean," Fargo said. He nodded at the rim. "Let me fetch my horse and we'll go see this earl."

"I'm at your disposal, kind sir," Flora responded, a devilish twinkle lighting her eyes.

Fargo knew an invite when he heard one. He climbed out of the gully, marveling at the odd twist of fate that had resulted in the encounter. It had been a spell since he last shared a bed with a woman, and the thought of Flora's ample bosom and shapely legs were enough to make his manhood rod-stiff. He held the Sharps in the crook of his left elbow, took the pinto's reins in his other hand, and ambled back.

Flora was waiting at the crest. "Are you sure it's safe to leave poor Jeems here?" she inquired. "We heard such awful tales about red savages and all kinds of fierce beasts that roam this terrible prairie, although we have yet to see any."

"Count yourself lucky," Fargo said. He spied a thin gray wisp of smoke rising to the northeast and pointed. "Is that your camp?"

"Must be. I'm afraid my sense of direction is all askew out here, but they did have a fire going when I went for my stroll."

Fargo led off, aware of her studying him intently. "What are you folks doing in this territory?"

"We're on a hunting expedition. The earl goes on one at least once a year. Africa, India, South America—I've been to all those places with him." Flora sighed wearily. "He must have the world's biggest collection of stuffed heads. Tigers, lions, elephants, rhinos—you name it, he has one hanging somewhere in his castle."

Fargo glanced at her to see if she was joking but found she was serious. "What are you, his maid?"

"Goodness gracious, no. I work for the countess, his wife. The salt of the earth, that sweet woman is. Too bad she didn't marry someone with a better temperament."

"You don't like the earl much, do you?"

"Let's just say that if I didn't think so highly of her nibs, I'd be back in England right this minute enjoying a cup of tea and some biscuits while reading the London *Times*," Flora said wistfully.

Although it wasn't Fargo's nature to pry, he wanted to learn a little more before meeting the distinguished couple. "Where are you headed?"

"I honestly don't know. Hadden isn't one to announce his intentions in advance."

"Hadden? Who is he?"

"I'm sorry. Ashley Hadden is the Earl of Somerset. Kendra, my mistress, is the Countess of Somerset. I've been in her employ going on five years now." Flora paused. "Sometimes it seems a lot longer."

"How many are there in your party?"

"All told, twenty-one."

The total was a lot higher than Fargo had thought would be the case, and he was about to ask why there were so many when the patter of onrushing footsteps to his rear warned him that the one called Jeems had recovered much sooner than he had anticipated. He whirled, or tried to. Iron arms looped around his waist and he was lifted bodily and slammed to the ground, losing his grip on the Sharps. He felt Jeems pounce on his back and winced when a knee gouged into his spine.

"Jeems!" Flora cried. "Stop!"

The enraged Englishman ignored her. Fists flailing, he pounded away at the back of Fargo's head. Fargo absorbed several blows before he could bunch his leg and stomach muscles and heave. Jeems tumbled off but rolled with the agility of an acrobat into a crouch. He aimed a vicious kick at Fargo's face, which Fargo evaded by jerking aside.

Shoving upright, Fargo barely had time to set himself before the manservant was on him again. This time Jeems assumed a boxing posture and flicked his left fist. Fargo blocked with a forearm, pivoted, and delivered a right to the gut that sent Jeems staggering.

Fargo tried to close in to finish Jeems off, but the man recovered swiftly. Rock-hard knuckles grazed Fargo's chin, and a follow-through clipped his cheek. Back-pedaling, Fargo traded punches, waiting for an opening he could exploit. It became apparent that Jeems was a skillful boxer, not one to make an obvious mistake. Fargo found it difficult to keep the slightly smaller man at bay.

From far away came shouts, signifying the people at the camp had observed the fight and were hurrying to the scene.

Flora was bellowing in unladylike fashion for Jeems to cease and desist.

Fargo shut both out of his mind and concentrated on the matter at hand. He had been in more than his share of saloon brawls and could hold his own against most anyone in a rough-and-tumble fight. But Jeems was a pugilist, a man who took his fisticuffs seriously, and now that his initial rage had subsided, he was circling Fargo, keeping out of reach while awaiting his chance to strike. Fargo couldn't simply charge, swinging wildly. He had to take his time, whittle his foe down.

Jeems tried a jab to the face that Fargo tipped aside. Pivoting, Fargo flicked a straight left at the manservant, and when Jeems elevated an arm to counter the blow, Fargo delivered a sweeping hook to the body that jolted Jeems from head to toe.

The Englishman backed off, scowling.

Suddenly Flora stepped between them and tried to give Jeems a shove. "Enough of this nonsense! Be civil, you brute!"

In response, Jeems pushed her so hard she stumbled into Fargo, who had to catch her to keep her from falling. The momentary distraction proved costly, as Jeems leaped in and connected with a punch to the head.

Dazed, Fargo got clear of Flora and set himself. Jeems attacked, pumping his arms, trying to overcome Fargo with a flurry of punches, but Fargo held his ground and landed several solid hits. Again they separated, Jeems breathing heavily.

To the northeast arose the thud of hoofbeats as riders approached at a gallop.

Fargo didn't dare take his eyes off the manservant to see who was coming. He stepped to his right, his fists clenched and ready. Jeems foolishly slid in close, feinted, and attempted to plant an uppercut on Fargo's jaw, but he was so obvious that Fargo was able to glide inside the uppercut

14

and rock the Englishman with a combination. Jeems tottered, his arms drooping.

Drawing back his right arm, Fargo swung a roundhouse that toppled the manservant like a poled ox. The crunch of his knuckles on the man's mouth was sweet music. Fargo stood over Jeems, waiting to learn if another punch was necessary. Except for the flutter of his eyelids, Jeems was still.

"You were magnificent," Flora breathed.

Fargo glanced at her. "A five-year-old Sioux would be tougher than this joker."

The drumming of hooves was almost upon them. Fargo turned at the same moment the foremost rider launched himself into the air. He glimpsed a sinewy man dressed in a brown suit, and then he was bowled over and the newcomer was striving to bash his brains in with the butt of a small pistol.

Only Fargo's lightning reflexes saved him. He dodged the first few blows, hooked his hands under the man's legs, and heaved. The man went flying. Fargo surged erect as he saw the man sit up and go to level his pistol.

Without a moment's hesitation, Fargo streaked his right hand to his Colt and cleared the six-shooter in a blur. The revolver boomed, the slug ripping into the man's shoulder and flattening him in the grass.

Whirling, Fargo confronted the half-dozen men on horseback who were slowing as they unlimbered their hardware. "Do it and you're dead!" he warned.

Flora uttered a terrified shriek. Dashing forward, frantically waving her arms, she screeched, "No! No! Put down your guns! You don't understand! He wasn't attacking us!"

A tall man in an immaculate suit and derby paused with a revolver half-drawn from a shoulder holster. He stared at Jeems, then at the redhead. "I demand an immediate explanation, Miss Livingstone. I distinctly saw this ruffian in buckskins assaulting Mr. Jeems."

"It wasn't that way at all, sir," Flora said timidly. "Jeems attacked him after he stopped Jeems—" she froze and gave a little cough, "—that is, after they had a minor disagreement."

"What was the nature of this disagreement?"

"It was nothing, sir, truly."

Fargo detected an underlying hint of fear in her voice and wondered why she didn't come right out and reveal the truth. He scanned the other riders to make sure none was trying to get a bead on him, then checked on the man he had shot, who was sitting up with a hand clasped to his wounded wing.

The tall man wasn't satisfied with Flora's answer. "Jeems is out cold and Oakley is sitting there with a bullet hole in him and you say it was over nothing?" His tone hardened. "You will provide more details, Miss Livingstone, this instant!"

"I'd rather not, sir."

So this was the nobleman, Fargo mused. He studied Ashley Hadden and did not like what he saw. Hadden's features were flinty, almost cruel, his eyes smoldering pools of arrogance. He had a tilt to his head, as if he were looking down his nose at the whole world. And when Hadden spoke, he did so in a dictatorial way.

Right at the moment the earl's face was a marble mask of anger. "I will not tolerate insubordinate behavior, especially in the hired help. You will account for your actions, please, and be quick about it, or I'll have you dismissed and sent back to England."

Her lower lip quivering, Flora said softly, "Jeems was having a go at me when this man came along and stopped him."

"Having a go?" Hadden repeated, blanching. "Am I to understand he was forcing himself on you?"

Flora replied in a strained whisper. "Yes, sir."

The earl's lips parted, exposing a neat row of small white teeth. "You swear this is the truth?"

"By all that is holy, yes, sir, I do."

The look that Hadden gave Jeems did not bode well for the manservant. "Mr. Moulton and Mr. Heath, I want the two of you to take Mr. Jeems back to camp. He is to be confined to his tent until I send for him."

"Yes, sir," said one of the men addressed, a beefy man with enormous sideburns.

Hadden focused on the wounded man. "Are you in much pain, Mr. Oakley?"

"Not much to speak of, governor." Oakley slowly stood. "It's nothing compared to the time that bloody Zulu put a spear into me." His right arm tucked to his side, he picked up his pistol with his other hand, then scrutinized Skye Fargo. "Never saw anyone as fast as you before, son. You could've killed me if you'd wanted to, couldn't you have?"

"Yes," Fargo admitted.

"Well then, I owe you my life. And I'm terribly sorry about the misunderstanding. I thought Miss Livingstone was in danger and acted without learning the facts first. My sincere apologies."

Fargo didn't quite know what to say. In all his wide-flung travels he'd never met anyone so outrageously polite. He'd shot the man, yet there Oakley stood smiling and offering an apology for the inconvenience!

The Earl of Somerset moved closer. "You will accompany us back to camp also, stranger, and give your account of the incident. When I'm satisfied that all the facts are known, you'll be free to leave."

Fargo couldn't resist a smirk as he stared up at the haughty nobleman. "I've got news for you, Hadden. I'm not going anywhere with you. The only fact worth mentioning is that I'm leaving. Adios." He slid the Colt into its holster, turned, and gripped the saddle horn.

"I insist that you come with us," the earl snapped.

"I don't work for you," Fargo responded, mounting. "So I do as I damn well please." He touched the brim of his hat to Flora and was set to ride off when the sight of another rider approaching rooted him in place.

The rider was another woman, but what a woman! Fargo had seldom seen anyone so exquisitely lovely. She had lustrous blond hair that cascaded over her shoulders in golden waves. Her eyes were a piercing green, her skin as smooth as the finest silk. Every feature was so perfectly sculpted, she seemed more like a work of art than a living, breathing human being. Her vibrant body was clothed in a full-length gown that clung to her sensuous limbs, accenting her feminine charms. Fargo gazed on her and felt his mouth go dry.

Reining up, the blond glanced at Hadden, then at Fargo. She blinked, as if in surprise, and seemed to make an effort to compose herself. "Would someone kindly tell me what is going on?" she asked in a musical voice.

"There's been a row, Kendra," Hadden answered. "It's nothing to bother your dainty head about, darling."

The Countess of Somerset's jaw twitched ever so slightly. "Why not let me be the judge of that, husband? My dainty head has handled crises before. And since from the look of things Flora is involved, I have every right to be privy to whatever has happened."

"It's nothing I can't handle," the earl said with an angry edge. He nodded at Fargo. "I simply have to convince this rotter that it's in his best interests to visit our camp and provide his version of events."

Kendra Hadden looked at Skye. "Is there a reason you won't grace us with your company, sir?"

"My handle is Fargo. Skye Fargo. And the reason is that uppity so-and-so sitting next to you, ma'am."

Sparkling laughter burst from the lady's rosy lips. She caught herself, grinned at her simmering husband, and bestowed a ravishing smile on Fargo. "Yes, Ashley does have a flair for antagonizing people. But I wish you would reconsider."

"I'm on my way to Denver," Fargo said lamely. Inwardly, he wanted nothing more than an chance to get to know this delightful beauty better, but his common sense told him that he'd be asking for a heap of trouble if he didn't curb his yearning.

"Surely Denver can wait a day or two?" Kendra countered. "We haven't seen a new face in ages, and we would welcome the chance to show what gracious hosts we can be."

Fargo couldn't imagine the earl as a gracious host under any circumstances, but he hesitated, tempted by her beauty.

"We would be most grateful."

The Earl of Somerset chose that moment to interject a comment. "If this blighter doesn't want to honor our simple request, let him go on his way. Who needs him!"

"We do," Kendra said, "if we're ever to find our way back to civilization."

"You're lost?" Fargo asked in amazement.

"Sort of," Kendra replied.

"Didn't you hire a guide?"

"Sort of," she said again.

Hadden made a gesture of impatience. "We can handle our problems without this plainsman's help." He began to wheel his mount.

"No, we can't," Kendra stood her ground. There was a heartfelt appeal in her eyes, and a hint of something else, as she said, "Please, Mr. Fargo."

Against his better judgment, and although he had an inkling of what he was letting himself in for, Skye Fargo said, "Lead the way, ma'am." He lifted the reins and hoped he wouldn't live to regret his decision.

2

The camp had been pitched in a wide hollow so the tents were below the level of the surrounding prairie, but that was the only sensible precaution the party had taken. The campfire was three times as big as it should be and was making enough smoke to lure every hostile within five miles. Forty horses were strung out on a single long picket rope that ran for dozens of yards, instead of being divided up and tethered to short ropes so Indians would find it harder to steal them. Two large wooden wagons used for transporting goods were parked at the west side of the encampment, instead of closer to the fire where they could serve as a line of defense against attack. And the tents themselves were scattered all over the hollow rather than being clustered together for mutual protection.

Fargo surveyed the site and commented, "Whoever this guide of yours is, he doesn't know beans from buffalo chips if you ask me."

Kendra gave her husband an I-told-you-so look. "I've been saying the same thing for weeks, but no one will listen to me."

"I admit Mr. Reardon has proven to be a disappointment," the earl remarked. "But he's brought us this far without mishap."

"How far would that be?" Fargo asked.

"We left Kansas City three weeks ago," Hadden disclosed. "Our original intention was to track down a herd of buffalo so I could bag myself a trophy bull. Apparently the number of these beasts has been vastly overstated, because as yet we've not seen a single one."

"There are millions roaming the plains," Fargo said. "I've come across hundreds in the past few days, some close to this very spot." He gazed around. "Have you been camped here long?"

"Goodness, no," Kendra responded. "We've been wandering around so much our horses are on their last legs."

The party had gathered to greet them. Fargo discovered one other female among the bunch, a black-haired woman wearing a prim brown dress who was nervously wringing a white handkerchief. She smiled in relief and came forward as they reined up.

"Thank the good Lord neither of you was hurt," she told the earl and the countess, completely ignoring the wounded man, Oakley, who was a dozen feet behind them.

"Skye Fargo," Kendra said, "permit me to introduce my sister-in-law, Elizabeth Hadden."

"Ma'am," Fargo said.

Elizabeth scrunched up her nose. "A commoner, aren't you? More's the pity."

"Pleased to meet you, too," Fargo said sarcastically.

Flora Livingstone was busy helping Oakley dismount. Two brawny men gathered up the horses, while another hurried up carrying a glass filled with water. He was skin and bones, his clothes so loose-fitting he resembled a scarecrow. Bowing, he held out the glass. "Some water for you, sir. All that activity in this dreadful heat is bound to have sapped your strength."

"Thank you, Hollis," the earl said, taking the glass and swallowing the contents in four great gulps. "How very decent of you."

Hollis smiled, bowed again, and hurried off.

Fargo said nothing, but he was disgusted by the slavish attitude of Hollis and the others. They acted as if the earl were their master, and they seemed downright proud to be at his beck and call. Fargo couldn't understand how anyone would allow themself to be lorded over that way.

The Sharps in hand, Fargo trailed the royal couple to a tent much larger than all the rest, standing apart, near the vans. A canopy attached to the front afforded shade, and under it several chairs and a small table had been set up.

Ashley Hadden took his seat as might someone perching on a golden throne. He poured another glass of water from a pitcher on the table and offered it to his sister, not his wife. She accepted it with a beaming smile. Hadden sat back and smoothed his jacket. "Now let us get to the matter at hand, shall we?"

"What about poor Oakley?" Kendra asked.

"Revis is already tending to him," Hadden said, indicating a tent to the south. He raised a hand and called out, "Bring Mr. Jeems!"

By now most of the group had converged on the main tent. Fargo stood to one side, watching a pair of guards escort a pale Jeems over. The manservant was trying hard to hide the sheer terror lurking inside him, but he was doing a poor job. The terror seemed unwarranted, since the worst that could happen would be his dismissal. Or so Fargo thought.

Jeems and Flora were made to stand in front of the Earl of Somerset. The nobleman regarded them balefully. "I want to get to the bottom of this, without delay, so I can devote myself to more pressing problems." He jabbed a finger at Flora. "Begin, please. And I want the truth and nothing but the truth."

"There's not much to tell, sir. Mr. Jeems and I went for a walk, he became too forward for my liking, and Mr. Fargo came to my rescue. That's all."

"Hardly," Hadden said. "You are aware, aren't you, of the standing order that no one is to go more than twenty yards from the camp unless they first receive permission?"

"Yes, sir."

"Yet you went off quite a way with Mr. Jeems, didn't you? Why did you go so far? What did you have in mind?"

"Nothing, sir, except to enjoy a stroll," Flora said defensively. "All of us are tired of being kept in camp whenever we stop. I just wanted to get out and about."

"Really?"

Everyone there caught the hidden meaning. Fargo hoped Flora would wade into the earl and give him a piece of her mind, but to his surprise it was the countess who bristled.

"That will be quite enough, Ashley! If Flora says she had perfectly innocent intentions, then she very well did. I will not have you impugn her integrity in front of the whole camp."

The earl forced a polite smile and said, "Such an idea

never entered my head, dearest. I'm merely trying to learn all the facts so my judgment will be fair." He cocked his head at the manservant. "What do you have to say for yourself, Mr. Jeems? Did you attempt to have your way with Miss Livingstone?"

"As I live and breathe, sir, never!" the manservant said. "We went for a stroll, true enough, and sat down to have a chat. And when I went to peck her on the cheek, friendly-like, she up and raised a fuss. The next thing I knew, that big bounder in buckskins was taking a rifle butt to my head."

Ashley Hadden swiveled toward Fargo. "And you, sir? What is your version of the incident? Which one of these two should I believe?"

"Both."

"Both?" Hadden repeated skeptically.

"Flora did go for a walk with Jeems, and Jeems did try to give her a peck," Fargo said.

"If that's all that happened, why did you assault him?"

"Because at the same time that he was giving her a kiss, he was also hiking her dress up to her neck and trying to pry her legs apart," Fargo detailed. "In this country a man doesn't do that to a woman against her will unless he's loco or fond of an early grave."

The nobleman faced his manservant. "Any rebuttal, Mr. Jeems?"

"He's lying!"

"Why? What is his motive?"

Jeems was rubbing his palms back and forth as if his hands were cold. "I don't know, governor. But I pledge by my sainted mother that—"

The Earl of Somerset snapped a hand up, causing the manservant to fall silent. "Please, Mr. Jeems. Don't insult your mother by linking her good name to this revolting incident." He scowled in disgust. "It's bad enough the two of you disobeyed me. But your behavior was a grave breach of proper conduct."

"Are you saying that you're taking his word over mine?" Jeems asked, pointing at Fargo.

"I have to go by the facts, and the facts in this case speak for themselves. This plainsman, as you yourself admitted, has no reason to lie. He saw you trying to take advantage of Miss Livingstone." Hadden paused. "My judgment is as follows: dismissal as soon as we reach a town, or forty lashes."

Fargo had been leaning on one of the support poles that held up the canopy. He had little interest in the proceedings and was devoting his time to admiring the countess on the sly. But on hearing lashes mentioned he straightened, looking at Jeems. The manservant had blanched and taken a short step forward.

"Please, sir. With all due respect, the punishment is hardly fair."

"Fair?" Hadden hissed. "In my estimation, I'm being quite lenient. I should simply set you afoot and let you find your own way out of this vast wasteland. Is that what you would prefer?"

Jeems gazed out over the waving ocean of grass and gulped. "No, sir. I wouldn't."

"Which will it be then? The decision is yours."

The answer came in a wavering croak. "If I was dismissed under these circumstances, I'd never be able to find work as a manservant again. I have no choice but to accept the forty lashes."

Hadden nodded curtly and stood. "You've all heard. And let this serve as a lesson. Decorum will be observed at all times, and those failing to do so will be punished. We simply must behave as proper Englishmen should." His chest puffed out. "You have a duty not only to me, your employer, but to your country as well. Just because we live among barbarians does not mean we stoop to their level."

Fargo had stomached just about all of Ashley Hadden he could abide. He was of half a mind to mount up and ride on out when Kendra Hadden glanced at him and gave him the sort of glowing, inviting smile that could light up a dark room. He smiled back, but she had already turned her head.

In the meantime the skinny Englishman named Hollis had appeared at the earl's side, a coiled whip clutched in one hand. Hadden took it and let the lash unwind at his feet. "Would two of you be so kind as to prepare Mr. Jeems?"

A pair of somber men advanced. One stripped the manservant from the waist up, then each took an arm and led Jeems over to a wagon. He didn't resist as his hands were lashed to either side of a wheel, leaving him in a stooped posture with his back fully exposed.

The earl strolled out from under the canopy, giving the whip a few flicks to limber his wrist. "Try to keep a stiff upper lip, Mr. Jeems," he said. "Do your heritage proud."

Fargo stayed where he was. He could see well enough. Kendra had not left her chair. Her hands were folded tightly at her waist, her spine rigid with tension, her elegant features downcast. Everyone else had moved off to see the whipping, leaving them temporarily alone. He stepped closer to her and said, "If you don't like to watch, why just sit there?"

"It's expected of me, Mr. Fargo."

"Call me Skye." He heard a loud crack and saw the earl taking practice swings. "Who expects you to? Him?"

"It's my station in life. Titles bring with them certain responsibilities."

"You don't sound too happy about it."

"I'm not." Kendra lowered her voice. "Truth is, I'm miserable. Have been for years."

"Can't blame you there," Fargo said. "Being married to that bastard would have anyone down in the dumps."

The countess faced him. "In England, using such language in my presence would be a serious breach of etiquette."

"This isn't England. Over here we say and do as we please."

"So I've noticed."

Their conversation was brought to an abrupt end by a piercing shriek. Ashley Hadden had applied the whip to Jeems and a great red welt now marred the manservant's back. Again the whip snaked out, the lash biting deep between the shoulder blades. Jeems arched his back and gritted his teeth, holding in his cry this time.

The assembled Britishers looked on without showing any emotion. Not a one made any move to interfere.

"How can they just stand there and let this happen?" Fargo wondered aloud.

"Mr. Jeems brought this on himself. They know that and respect the earl's verdict." Kendra grimaced as another stroke was delivered. "If you don't approve, why don't you put a stop to it?"

"I'm an outsider here. It's none of my affair." He locked his eyes on hers. "If it wasn't for you, I'd be miles away by now."

"What do you mean?"

"You know darn well what I mean."

The countess averted her face. "You shouldn't talk like that, Skye. You know I'm a married woman, and a lady."

"I've only known you fifteen minutes, and it's as plain as the nose on your face that you're as unhappily married as they come," Fargo responded. "As for being a lady, a woman is still a woman no matter what she goes around calling herself."

"What are you implying?"

"I saw the way you looked at me that first time. You're as attracted to me as I am to you."

"Rubbish!" Kendra said, flushing. "It's easy to see that you're no gentleman!" Rising, she went to join the watchers.

Fargo shrugged and leaned against the pole again. He caught Elizabeth Hadden giving him the kind of spiteful stare she might give a bug she had found in her bloomers. When she realized he had noticed, she promptly looked away.

All this time the Earl of Somerset had been applying the lash to Jeems with a skill that hinted at lots of prior experience. Thin strips of skin were peeled away with every stroke, and by now bloody rivulets trickled down the man's back. Jeems had gone slack, whining at each blow.

Fargo turned away in disgust and happened to set eyes on a small tent just as the front flap parted and a grizzled man in grimy buckskins, scuffed boots, and a floppy hat with holes in it stepped out. Reardon, Fargo guessed, as the man walked unsteadily in his direction. He smelled the alcohol long before Reardon reached him.

"Howdy, stranger. Where'd you come from?"

"Just happened by," Fargo said. They introduced themselves to one another, then Reardon's bloodshot eyes shifted to the earl.

"So the son of a bitch is at it again. You'd think his arm would give out on him after a while."

"He does this a lot?"

"Four times since I signed on to find game for this sorry outfit," Reardon said. "If I'd known what I was letting myself in for, I would have stayed in Kansas City." Smacking his lips, he said, "Say, you wouldn't happen to have some coffin varnish in your saddlebags, would you? I could go for a swig of whiskey right about now."

"A man who brings booze on the trail is asking for trouble," Fargo replied.

"A swallow or two every now and then never hurts." Reardon scratched the stubble on his pointed chin. "Used up the last of mine last night. Been nursing that bottle for over a week."

"The earl doesn't object to your drinking?"

Reardon grinned slyly. "I reckon he would if he caught me in the act, but so far I've been too canny for him."

The punishment was about at an end. The earl applied five more strokes, none of which elicited a sound because Jeems had passed out. Slowly coiling the whip, Hadden barked orders at the same two men who had tied Jeems up. They swiftly freed him and carted the limp manservant toward a tent.

Hadden returned to his chair, a slight strut in his walk. Breathing heavily from the exertion, he sat down and gulped water. Kendra and Elizabeth took their seats on either side of him.

Reardon winked at Fargo, then declared, "I reckon you taught him, Your Highness."

A shadow passed over the earl's countenance. "How many times must I tell you not to call me that, Mr. Reardon? My title limits me to being addressed as 'sir'. Nothing more." He set his glass down. "On another matter, I'm glad you finally decided to join us. I thought you might sleep the day through. Again."

"What if I did? I was out all day yesterday hunting for buffalo and didn't get in 'til late."

"You always have an excuse, don't you?" Hadden said sharply. "Frankly, I'm tired of them. As tired as I am of roaming this damnable prairie without finding any game."

"It takes time," Reardon said.

"You have run out of time."

"What?"

"Mr. Fargo has informed us there are plenty of buffalo in our vicinity. You have twenty-four hours to find them or you can collect your pay and head on back to Kansas City."

"Now hold on, mister," Reardon said gruffly. "I don't know where you get off telling me my business. I scouted for the army for pretty near ten years and I know these plains as well as any man. If this Fargo character claims there are buffalo around, he's a blamed liar."

Whatever else the former scout might have said was lost to posterity when Fargo landed a roundhouse right to the chin that sent Reardon stumbling backward. The man kept his balance, though, then reached behind him to draw a large butcher knife from its sheath. Crouching, he wagged the gleaming blade and said, "I'm going to cut you to ribbons, you son of a bitch!"

The earl jumped up. "Hear now! I'll have none of this!"

Reardon ignored the command and rushed forward, swinging in wide arcs.

Fargo retreated, backing toward the tent. When his back brushed the canvas, he stopped, gauging the scout's next swing. A quick leap sideways enabled him to evade the knife, which ripped into the canvas. He slid in close, intending to grab Reardon's wrist and hold the knife at bay, but the scout was too fast for him, yanking the blade out and whirling.

"Stop it this instant!" Kendra Hadden cried.

The words were wasted. Sheer fury animated Reardon as he attacked, spearing the knife at Fargo's gut.

Fargo back-pedaled, dropped into a crouch, and came up holding his Arkansas toothpick. He parried a thrust, then retaliated with a slash across the forearm that sliced through the scout's buckskin sleeve and drew blood.

Suddenly cautious, Reardon circled to the right. He lunged low, going for Fargo's leg.

Fargo jumped aside. He could tell that Reardon wasn't a skilled knife-fighter, which in a way made the man even more dangerous. Inexperienced fighters were unpredictable, often attacking wildly, their very recklessness working to their advantage. Fargo stayed just out of reach, parrying stabs. Their blades rang in the quiet that had descended.

Out of the corner of one lake-blue eye, Fargo glimpsed the countess. She was riveted in place, a dainty hand at her throat, her eyes wide with concern. For who? Him?

The distraction nearly cost Fargo his life. Reardon took an unexpected hop, lancing his weapon at Fargo's midsection. A last-second twist spared Fargo, and as the blade whisked by his stomach he drove an elbow into the scout's nose.

Reardon backed off, spraying crimson drops all over the flattened grass. He tried pinching his nose with his free hand to stop the flow of blood, but some got into his eyes.

Fargo took immediate advantage. He took a swift stride, then jumped straight into the air and kicked, planting his boot on the scout's jaw.

Reardon was knocked a dozen feet and crashed onto his back. He tried once to rise, sputtered, and collapsed.

Quickly Fargo stripped the butcher knife from the scout's hand and tossed it over by the earl's chair. Hadden glared at it, then at him.

"Has anyone ever told you that you have a short temper, Mr. Fargo?"

"Temper has nothing to do with it." Fargo said. "In the West no man worth his salt will stand still for an insult. Keep that in mind or you might wind up going back to England minus a few teeth."

"Was that a threat?" the earl demanded.

"I'm just telling you the way things are," Fargo said. "Most every man you'll meet out here feels the same way."

"Ah. It's a matter of pride, is it?"

"Partly. Mainly it's just about being a man."

"Fascinating," the earl said. "The more I learn of your primitive country, the more enthralled I become." He poured another glass of water, then walked over to Reardon and unceremoniously upended it into the scout's open mouth.

Reardon sat bolt upright, coughing and spitting. He saw Fargo and his eyes scoured the nearby grass for his knife.

Failing to spot it, he started to rise, his right hand lowering toward his revolver.

"Are you that sure of yourself?" Fargo asked, his own hand inches from the butt of his six-shooter.

No one moved or spoke for the span of ten seconds. Reardon was sorely tempted to try; everyone could see that much. But he slowly shook his head and straightened. "No sirree. There will be another time."

"Not for you," Hadden declared. "You'll be too busy searching for buffalo." The scout opened his mouth to object but the earl cut him off. "I think I finally understand why you insisted on being paid by the day rather than receiving a flat sum, Mr. Reardon. I suspect you have been dragging your heels to increase your fee. Well, no more. You have twenty-four hours in which to find me the biggest bloody bull buffalo on this continent, or I will send you packing with only a small retainer for your time and services."

The scout clenched his fists and made as if to launch himself at the earl. He stopped when a dozen men stepped forward, ready to pounce if he dared lay a finger on the nobleman. Balefully glowering at them all, Reardon pivoted and tromped off toward the horses, saving his parting glance for the man who had beaten him.

Skye Fargo knelt and slid the toothpick into the sheath strapped to his right ankle. He hadn't been there an hour yet, and already he'd made a mortal enemy. Was his interest in the countess worth all the bother? he asked himself. Looking up, he caught her gaze and held it until she blushed slightly and hastened into the tent.

Yes, Fargo reflected with a grin, it most definitely was.

3

"Hold up there, handsome!"

Skye Fargo was strolling about the encampment when he was hailed. He stopped and waited for Flora Livingstone to overtake him, then together they kept on walking.

"I wanted to thank you for coming to my defense," the redhead said, touching his hand. "If not for you, the earl would have taken Jeems's word over mine."

"All I did was tell the truth," Fargo responded.

Her shoulder brushed against him. "Handsome *and* honest. You're not by any chance married, are you?"

"I'm not the marrying kind."

"Too bad," Flora said. She clasped her hands behind her back and took a deep breath, her breasts swelling against her blouse. "Smell that grass? Sometimes it reminds me of the heath. Makes me think of my childhood on the farm."

"Somehow I can't picture you slopping hogs."

Flora laughed. "My parents raised cattle. But you're right. Early on I decided the farming life wasn't for me. So off I went to London to seek fame and fortune." Her expression became rueful. "I wound up cleaning homes for a living, and then moved on to be a maid, and finally to working for the royals. At a reception I met the countess and have been with her ever since."

"Why does her husband treat her the way he does?"

Flora halted and checked to insure no one was within earshot. "It's not proper for me to be talking about the earl behind his back, but I simply can't stand the man. He treats his snob of a sister better than he does sweet Kendra."

"Why?"

"It was a marriage of convenience, on both sides. Kendra's parents were keen on having her acquire a title, and Ashley's father insisted he wed a decent lady and not the trollops he usually spent his time with."

"So neither one loves the other?"

"Ashley despises her. Kendra has tried her best to be a good wife, but he snubs her at every turn. I've lost track of the number of times I've found her weeping into her pillow." Flora clucked like an irate mother hen. "The poor, poor dear. She is utterly wretched."

"Why doesn't she get a divorce?" Fargo asked.

Flora did a double take. "That's just not done in polite English society, Skye. Why, the scandal would ruin her." She sadly gazed at the huge tent. "No, I'm afraid Kendra is stuck with her fate. She'll grow old, wither, and die, a lonely, heartbroken woman."

"And there's no way out for her?"

"Only one. Should the earl die, she'd be free to marry again as she chooses. Unfortunately Ashley is as healthy as a horse and will probably live forever."

Fargo said nothing and started walking. He took only a few steps when the pounding of hooves heralded the return of Reardon, who had been gone less than thirty minutes. Fargo figured the scout was racing back in such a hurry because he'd come across buffalo, but the agitated look on Reardon's face told a different story.

The scout reined up in a flurry of dust in front of the earl's tent and dashed inside without so much as a by-your-leave.

"Now what is that all about?" Flora asked.

"Let's find out."

Before they could get there, Ashley Hadden and Reardon appeared, the former holding a rifle, the latter gesturing excitedly. Hadden bellowed and men came running from all directions.

"What's all the excitement about?" Fargo inquired as he joined them.

"Indians," the earl said.

"That's right," Reardon declared. "I spotted a war party a long ways off. Must have been fifteen or twenty bucks, I reckon. They were headed this way."

Hadden was loading his rifle. "We'll ride out in force

and meet these savages. If they're looking for trouble, we'll give them a thrashing they won't soon forget."

"Hold on a second," Fargo cautioned. "It'd be best to make sure they're hostile before you go getting them all riled." He stared at the scout. "If they were so far off, how do you know it's a war party?"

"What else could it be?" Reardon replied stiffly.

"It might be a hunting party. Do you know which tribe they belonged to?"

"Couldn't tell."

The earl set the stock of his rifle on the ground. "I gather you don't think we should confront the red devils, Mr. Fargo?"

"Not until you know their intentions. They could be only after buffalo. If so, they might leave you alone if you leave them alone." Fargo hitched at his gun belt. "I'll ride out and have a look. You keep your hardware handy and post guards."

"Mr. Reardon will have to go with you to show you where he saw them," Hadden said.

The scout was clearly not any too happy about doing so, but he didn't argue. Scowling, he marched to his bay and mounted. "Hurry it up, mister."

Fargo made for the picket rope. As he went around the corner of the tent he glanced back and saw Kendra Hadden materialize at the front flap. She smiled encouragement, then gave a little wave. The earl noticed but showed no re-action.

Once on the Ovaro, Fargo trotted northward and fell in alongside Reardon. "Lead the way," he directed, then delib-erately let the bay gain a few yards on the Ovaro so he could keep an eye on Reardon at all times. Fargo knew he couldn't afford to turn his back to the scout, not if he wanted to keep on breathing. To be on the safe side he loosened the Colt in its holster and placed his hand on his waist, close to the grip.

Golden sunlight bathed the rustling grass. From the northwest wafted a cool wind containing a hint of moisture. Rain was coming, Fargo deduced, and hoped they wouldn't be caught in a thunderstorm.

"How far to where you saw them?" Fargo asked.

"Five miles, give or take," Reardon said sullenly.

The only sounds were the creak of well-worn saddle leather and the thud of heavy hooves. Fargo spied a few dark-gray clouds framing the western skyline, as yet nothing to worry about. Now and then he would rise in the stirrups to scour the prairie for the Indians, but each time he saw nothing except the unending expanse of open plain.

A mile and a half had fallen by the wayside when Fargo distinguished a large group of riders in the distance, heading straight for them. He drew rein, placed the Sharps across his thighs with the hammer cocked, and patiently waited.

Reardon had also halted. He shucked his rifle and fed a bullet into the chamber. "This is outright dumb," he complained. "We don't know who these redskins are. What if they're Sioux? They'll take our hair and stake us out to die."

Fargo didn't bother to mention that he had lived among the Sioux at one time and considered several of them close friends. He sat and studied the Indians until he could identify them by their dress and the style in which they wore their hair. "These are Arapahos," he revealed.

"Which isn't much better," Reardon groused. "They're friends of the Cheyenne, aren't they? And the Cheyenne have been kicking up their heels of late." He went to lift his rifle. "Maybe if I pick off a few they'll skedaddle."

Fargo leaned over and slapped the barrel down. "You'll sit still and keep your mouth shut."

The scout was furious but he held his temper in check.

Fifty yards out, the sixteen Arapahos had stopped for a conference. A bronzed warrior boasting three eagle feathers in his hair was doing most of the talking. At a word from him the others spread out. Then he came on alone, his hands held with palms outward to show his peaceful intentions.

Fargo observed that none of the braves had rifles or pistols. It was a hunting party, just as he had thought. He brought his right hand in front of his neck, his index and second fingers pointing upward, his other fingers clenched, and raised the hand in front of his head. This was sign language for "friend."

The oncoming warrior did likewise. Eight yards out he

drew rein, his hands flowing swiftly as he signed, "I am Eagle Claw, white-faced man. I speak for my brothers. We want to know why you are here."

"For the same reason you are. To hunt buffalo," Fargo answered.

"Just the two of you?"

"No. There are many more in our party," Fargo disclosed, adding for effect, "more than there are with you." Having lived among Indians, he knew how their minds worked, knew that if the Arapahos believed they could attack with impunity, they'd do so.

The warrior pondered that bit of news. "Where are these others?"

"Not far."

"Show us," Eagle Claw demanded.

Fargo wasn't about to let himself be bossed around. Complying would be taken as a sign of weakness, which all Indians were quick to exploit. So he responded, "Another time. We are looking for buffalo and must keep going."

"We hunt them also. You should join us."

The invitation seemed friendly enough, but Fargo was too savvy to fall for the ruse. The Arapahos would be all smiles and as nice as could be for a while. Then, the moment he lowered his guard, they'd pounce. "Your offer is kind. But we hunt alone."

Eagle Claw grunted, a sign of disapproval. "Very well. Perhaps we will meet again, white-eye." Yanking on the reins, he wheeled his pony and galloped westward, the rest falling in behind him.

"You should have let me plug the varmint," Reardon complained. "I saw that look in his eyes. There's going to be hell to pay."

"They're not stupid. The earl's party outnumbers them and has guns. They won't attack."

"Wishful thinking, if you ask me."

"I didn't," Fargo said curtly, his attitude short not just because of the scout's attitude. Deep down he had to admit that Reardon might be right, and if so he had put the English party in grave risk by permitting the Arapahos to leave unchallenged. Even so, he couldn't just shoot the warriors down in cold blood. It went against the grain.

All the way back to the camp, Fargo kept scouring the plain for signs of the band but saw none. In itself that meant little. The Arapahos were skilled stalkers; if they didn't care to be spotted, they wouldn't be. Not until it was too late.

The hollow bustled with activity as the earl's staff busied itself preparing the evening meal. A long table had been set up under the canopy and covered with a white cloth. Fine china and silver had been laid out. Crystal goblets stood beside each plate. Thick candles in ornate holders had been positioned near each end of the table for use after sunset.

A side panel on one of the vans had been opened, revealing all the conveniences of a modern kitchen: a stove, a cutting board, a barrel of water roosting over a sink, and all the utensils a cook could want.

Fargo guided the pinto to the picket line and was climbing down when the doleful state of the other horses gave him pause. Nearly all were hanging their heads, their sides coated with sweat, their dry mouths slack. He'd witnessed the same signs too many times not to know the cause, and recollected a comment made earlier by the countess.

Hitching his stallion, Fargo took the Sharps with him. He found the earl in the company of Reardon. Both of them stopped talking as he drew near. "You have a problem."

"So I gather," the nobleman said. "Ben Reardon has filled me in on your meeting with the Arapahos. He's of the opinion you should have shot a few to discourage them from causing us problems later."

"And what if they were only part of a bigger band?" Fargo asked. "Kill a few and you'd have the whole tribe out for your blood. No, we did the right thing." He cradled the rifle in both arms. "I'm more worried about those horses of yours. They're in bad shape."

The Earl of Somerset showed genuine concern. "I know. They're English-bred, the best money can buy. But they haven't fared well on this terrible prairie, even with all the grass there is to eat."

Fargo nodded. "I could see they're not run-of-the-mill cayuses. How long has it been since they've had any water?"

"Three days."

"Then you'd better hope we find some tomorrow, or you'll wear out your shoe leather long before you reach Kansas City!"

Hadden gazed at the string of horses and asked mildly, "Am I to understand that despite all that's happened you intend to stick around a while longer to help us out of our dilemma?"

"No!" was on the tip of Fargo's tongue. He didn't care one way or the other what happened to the nobleman. But he had taken a shine to Flora, and he would do all in his power to protect the countess Kendra. For their sake, and theirs alone, he said, "I reckon I'll stay for a while yet."

"Thought you might, old chap," Hadden said, smiling enigmatically.

Ben Reardon placed both hands on his hips. "We don't need him, sir. I can do the job just fine by myself."

"Like you have been doing?" Hadden asked. "Please don't insult my intelligence. Until Mr. Fargo came along, you played all of us for fools so you could fatten your wallet. If I thought for a minute that I could persuade him to serve as our guide on this expedition . . ." He stopped and glanced expectantly at Skye.

Fargo shook his head. Helping them out of a tight fix was one thing. Putting up with the earl, day after day over a long period, was another. It would stretch his self-control to its limits and result in no end of trouble. He'd rather be strung up by his thumbs over a hot fire.

Hadden sighed. "Yes, well, as I was saying . . . if I thought I could hire Mr. Fargo, I would give you the boot, Mr. Reardon, and file a formal complaint with your government about your actions to date."

"The government?" Reardon repeated in dismay. "What do they have to do with anything?"

"I'm in this charming country not only on holiday but as an official representative of Her Majesty's government, and I will be stopping in Washington on my way home." The earl had the look of a cat about to devour a mouse. "A few words in the right ears and you would never scout for anyone again."

Fargo saw fleeting panic ripple across Reardon's grizzled face and wondered why the scout was so upset. The government couldn't do anything to him unless it could prove he had swindled the earl's party, which would be next to impossible. Yes, Reardon had failed to find buffalo, but that in itself wasn't a crime. So why did Reardon look so panic-stricken?

The scout's cocky attitude had deflated like a punctured balloon. "What if I make it up to you?" he now asked.

"How?" Hadden wanted to know.

"By finding you what you want. The biggest damn buffalo in all creation."

"You should have done that weeks ago."

"It's not as easy as you think." The scout regained some of his testy disposition. "So what if there are millions of buffalo roaming the prairie? You want a bull that's not run-of-the-mill, a trophy beast as you keep calling him. And even Fargo will have to admit they're harder to find."

The Earl of Somerset looked at Fargo, who nodded.

"Very well," Hadden said. "I'll give you the benefit of the doubt for the time being. But what I said earlier still goes. Find me one by tomorrow night, or I'll make you sorry you were ever born!"

"That's all I ask," Reardon said. "You watch, Your Highness. I'll get me a good night's sleep and be off at first light." So saying, he spun on his heel and made for his tent.

Hadden snickered in contempt. "Quite a remarkable specimen, what? He's as fickle as the wind." Turning, he clapped Fargo on the back and said, "Now, how about a meal fit for a king? Literally." He adopted a wide smile. "I would be grateful if you would be the guest of honor at our table tonight."

Fargo couldn't quite believe his ears. All day long the earl had treated him as if he were pond scum. Now suddenly the nobleman had done a complete turnaround and acted as if he wanted to be the best of friends. When it came to being fickle, the Earl of Somerset had Ben Reardon beat all hollow.

"What do you say, chap?" Ashley Hadden persisted. "I've already taken the liberty of telling my darling wife you were to be invited, and she's *so* looking forward to having you join us."

Was it Fargo's imagination or did he detect a crafty

gleam in the earl's eyes? Although suspicious, he couldn't pass up the chance to talk to the countess again. "Fine by me," he responded.

"Most excellent," Hadden declared happily. "You can make yourself presentable and join us in half an hour." Humming to himself, he walked off.

If there was a valuable lesson Skye Fargo had learned during his wanderings, it was to treat life like a poker hand. Just like a gambler, a person should always keep his cards close to his vest, never trust the other players, and be as good at reading people as he was at reading hands.

Fargo sure as hell didn't trust the earl. He suspected Hadden was playing his cards close to the vest, although he was unable to read the nobleman's motive. Until he stumbled on a clue, he figured he would just take the cards as they were dealt.

The earl had said to make himself presentable, so Fargo dabbed his face and neck with his bandanna and brushed some of the dust off his boots. To kill time he ambled around the encampment, and on rounding a tent nearly collided with a man coming the other way.

"I say, sir! That was close!" Oakley exclaimed cheerfully.

Fargo indicated the man's sling. "How's the shoulder?"

"Couldn't be better. The bullet missed the bone and there was little bleeding. The doctor says I'll be good as new in two months."

"There's a doctor with this outfit?"

"I should say so. The earl never goes anywhere without his personal physician, Revis." Oakley paused. "Not to mention his groom, valets, cook, horseman, and all the rest."

Fargo was beginning to appreciate why the earl's party was so big. "Where do you fit into the scheme of things?"

"I'm one of his bodyguards," Oakley said proudly. "He never goes anywhere without the five of us by his side." He chuckled. "Not that the earl needs us. He's a crack pistol- and rifle-shot. He studied swordsmanship under the Duke of Normandy himself. And he was taught the manly art of self-defense by a member of the Japanese consulate in London. There isn't a more lethal man alive."

"The earl?" Fargo said in disbelief. It had been his opinion the nobleman was about as dangerous as a feisty praying mantis.

"Don't let his lean looks fool you," Oakley cautioned. "The man is the devil incarnate when he's aroused."

"Has a temper, does he?" Fargo asked, having already guessed that much for himself.

"I shouldn't be talking about him this way," Oakley said softly. "But between the two of us, he has the worst temper of any human being I've ever met."

"Does he hit the staff when he's mad?"

"On occasion."

"How about his wife? Does he beat the countess, too?"

The bodyguard stiffened indignantly. "I think we've covered all of this subject we need to cover." He nodded at the Colt. "And don't forget. I would enjoy learning the tricks of your fast-draw before you leave us."

Fargo watched Oakley leave, mulling over the new facts he had gleaned. In his mind's eye he pictured the earl savagely pounding on the countess, and he quivered with rage. It didn't matter if Hadden had a fancy title or not, no man had the right to go around beating women.

Several people had gathered at the long table, so Fargo went over. Flora was there and introduced Fargo to the physician, Revis, to Hollis, the groom, and to Moulton, one of the bodyguards who would be joining them that evening.

Flora also steered Fargo to a chair near the right end of the table and gave him a sly wink as she did so. Fargo had no idea why until a few moments later when the earl, the countess, and the earl's sister emerged, dressed in their finest clothes, and it turned out his chair was right next to Kendra's.

Elizabeth Hadden gave Fargo a chilly stare, but her brother was smiling like a snake-oil salesman. By contrast, Kendra seemed unduly nervous.

"Welcome, all of you!" Hadden said. "And a special welcome to our special guest, Mr. Fargo."

"Here, here," the doctor and Moulton both said.

During the six-course meal Fargo was plied with questions about life in the West. The earl, in particular, soaked up information like a sponge. Elizabeth Hadden refused to make a single comment all evening. The countess made few herself, even though Fargo tried to draw her into conversation several times.

By the end of dessert Fargo was disgusted with the whole situation and of half a mind to saddle up and ride out in the morning. His main reason for staying had been Kendra Hadden, and it was now plain that despite her earlier interest she wanted nothing to do with him.

Later, as Fargo was toting his saddle, bedroll, and rifle to a secluded spot where he could sleep undisturbed, he heard light footsteps behind him and spun, only to find it was Flora Livingstone. "What do you want?" he asked.

"Is that any way to greet a girl who's come to gaze at the stars with you?"

"I'm not in the mood for staring at the sky," Fargo informed her, depositing his gear on the ground.

"What a marvelous coincidence," Flora said impishly. "Neither am I." With that, she took a brazen step, molded her body to his, and kissed him full on the lips.

4

The night had suddenly taken a whole new turn. Skye Fargo felt the redhead's teeth nibble lightly on his lower lip and inhaled the minty fragrance of her hair. He cupped her buttocks and heard her moan softly deep in her throat. When they broke for air, she giggled girlishly and pushed back.

"What you must think of me!"

"That depends. Are you playing games?" Fargo asked, remembering Jeems.

"Not on your life, handsome," Flora said. "I've wanted you from the moment I laid eyes on you." She stepped close again and placed a palm flat on his thigh. "Do you have any idea how long it's been since I last had a man? The bloody earl doesn't let the staff fraternize." She spat out the last word distastefully.

"Aren't you taking a chance being seen with me?"

Flora grinned. "That's where I'm hoping your Yankee ingenuity will come in handy."

Fargo looked around. He had picked a spot near the horses so he could keep an eye on the Ovaro. The nearest tent was thirty feet away and it was dark, a sign the occupants had gone to sleep. No one else was anywhere near. But at his insistence the earl had posted a guard, and the man was at the opposite end of the camp, smoking a cigarette while walking the perimeter. Eventually the sentry would come around to their side. He needed somewhere a little more private.

"Well?" Flora teased.

Fargo suddenly swooped her into his arms, whirled, and dashed into the high grass. Flora squealed, then put a hand to her mouth to stifle her laughter. After going forty yards,

Fargo gently set her down and reclined at her side. "Will this do?" he whispered.

"Wonderfully," Flora said, coiling a slender arm around his neck to pull him close. She stopped when their lips were almost touching. "Wait a minute. What about those horrible redskins you were telling us about at supper?"

"They rarely attack at night."

"How often is rarely?"

"There's no cause to worry," Fargo said. "If they try anything, it won't be until morning."

"Well, if you say so, luv." Flora started to kiss him, but once more she stopped. "What about snakes? There aren't any great bleeding snakes in this grass, are there?"

"You talk too damn much," Fargo growled, lowering his mouth to hers. She gave a contented sigh and melted, her breasts pressing against his chest, her hands roving through his hair. Fargo slipped his tongue between her cherry lips and swirled it against hers.

For both of them, the need had gone too long unfulfilled. The longer they kissed, the more their sexual hunger showed. Their hands were everywhere. They couldn't get enough of each other, and it was hard to say which one of them was the more passionate.

Fargo unfastened her blouse while lathering her neck with kisses and then sucking on her earlobes. His fingers slipped inside her clothes, tracing lightly over her skin. A deft yank and Fargo had freed one of her breasts. He eased his hungry lips to her hard nipple and twirled it while she squirmed and cooed in sheer delight.

After a while Fargo turned to her other globe and gave it the same slow treatment. At the same time his hand glided lower, over her full hips to the junction of her legs. He pressed, eliciting a throaty purr. Then he worked his hand down and eased it under her skirt, where it feasted on her silken legs, rubbing them from thigh to knee, letting the friction build before he moved to the next stage.

Flora wriggled and groaned, her eyes closed, her nails digging into his back. Every so often she would pant and arch her back. "Yes, luv! Like that! Do that again!"

Fargo dallied at her creamy thighs. He stripped off her

underthings to gain access to her womanhood, and once he did the heady fragrance of her earthy scent tantalized him.

Propping her willowy legs apart, Fargo nuzzled her legs, her bush, and her nether lips. She was drenched, and when his darting tongue found her inner knob, she arched her back and gasped with joy.

"Oh, yes! Do me some more!"

Reaching up, Fargo squeezed her breasts while simultaneously flicking his tongue in her core. She bucked up off the ground as if trying to take flight, her legs pressing against his head so hard he could barely breathe. He kissed and stroked, bringing her to a fever pitch.

Then Fargo got a lovely surprise. Flora pulled his head up, shifted, and reached for his pants. Wearing a lecherous smirk, she unfastened his buckskins and yanked, exposing his rigid pole. Licking her lips, she edged closer.

The exquisite sensation was almost more than Fargo could bear. He gripped her hair and closed his eyes, savoring the building ecstasy. Bending, he swooped his hands past her ribs and grabbed hold of her breasts, which excited her so much she tried to inhale him.

Fargo pulled her up and planted his lips on hers. His middle finger explored her nether crack, gliding inside. Flora bit on his shoulder, then raked him with her nails. He began pumping his finger, and she cooperated by moving her bottom in rhythm.

"You do make a girl feel good," she remarked, her eyelids hooded.

"I'm just getting started," Fargo said. To prove his point he drove his pole into her, to the hilt.

Flora groaned. In order to heighten her pleasure, she hooked both ankles on Fargo's shoulders and ground into him with abandon.

Fargo paced himself, unwilling to end it so soon after so long. His strokes were precise and powerful. Flora huffed softly, striving to keep up with him. Their bellies slapped together; her breasts rubbed his chest.

Breathing deeply, Fargo held back the pending explosion in his loins. He wanted her to reach the pinnacle first, as she soon would if her unbridled moans were any indication. He kissed her to prevent her cries from being overheard by the guard, and continued kissing her as their bodies moved in harmony.

When the blast came, it curled Fargo's toes. Flora erupted first, her hips dancing wildly, panting in his ear as he held her close. On feeling her climax, he did too, his face fire-red, his body corded with muscle. A tingle rippled down his spine. He pumped until he couldn't pump any longer, until his arms and legs were weary and he was caked with perspiration, then he collapsed on top of her.

Flora grunted, then bit him again. "My, my, big man. That was impressive."

Fargo lay slumped on her breasts, catching his breath.

"You wouldn't happen to have a drop of English blood by any chance?" Flora joked softly.

"Doubt it."

"Must be all this wilderness living. Does wonders for the constitution."

Fargo patted her fanny and said, "Hush. The snakes will hear you."

Flora giggled, then pinched him. "Too bad I don't know anyone like you back in England. But then, you're not really interested in me, are you?"

"I'd like to just lie here quietly."

"No doubt. But we really must have a chat. I know you're hot up for the countess, and I should warn you to be almighty careful. You could cause her a lot of misery."

"Don't worry. I'm not about to give the earl another reason to beat her."

"You know about that?" Flora made her clucking sound again. "More's the pity. But at least now you can see why you must not do anything that would give the earl cause to suspect she's been unfaithful. Believe me, Skye, when I say he's not above thrashing her to within an inch of her life."

"And she'd stand there and take it?"

"What else can she do? I told you before that divorce is out of the question."

"Something should be done," Fargo said, but did not elaborate. Rolling off Flora, he dressed, then rose high enough to peer over the top of the grass. The guard was on the far side of the camp, strolling along as if he didn't have a care in the world. "Idiot," Fargo muttered.

"I beg your pardon?" Flora said, arranging her skirt.

"The earl's men are going to learn the hard way not to take Indians lightly." Fargo looked at her. "Do you have a gun?"

"Goodness gracious! What would I do with a bloody gun?"

"Protect yourself if we're attacked."

Flora tittered. "I wouldn't know the first thing about using a firearm. My best defense is the loudest scream you've ever heard. It'll bring all you strapping males rushing to my rescue."

Once Flora had put herself back together, Fargo took her hand and they walked back.

"I'd like to stay a while," Flora said, "but if the earl sees us together, he might become upset. Not fitting, and all that." She gave him a peck on the cheek and hurried off.

"Hey!" Fargo whispered, remembering something.

"What?"

"If you're so worried about my getting the countess into hot water, why did you seat me next to her at supper?"

"That wasn't my idea. She asked me to." Flora giggled as she hustled off.

There was a lot for Fargo to think about as he prepared to bed down. He would never have guessed the countess gave a hoot about him after the cold way she had treated him during the meal. It must have been an act, he mused, put on for her husband's benefit. His cause wasn't hopeless after all.

Then there was the earl himself. Fargo was puzzled by the nobleman's drastic change in attitude. It made no sense for Hadden to despise him one minute and treat him as a best friend the next. The earl had to be up to no good. But what did the devious bastard have up his sleeve?

Fargo placed the Sharps at his side and reclined with his head resting on his saddle. He drew the Colt, holding it in his right hand on his chest, and pulled the blanket up over his arm so the six-shooter was concealed. Even though he was sleeping out in the open, he wasn't overly concerned. There was no moon, so he was deep in shadow. And being a light sleeper, he'd awaken at the least little noise. On top of all that, he was near the Ovaro, and the stallion would alert him to anyone or anything trying to creep close to the camp.

In due course Fargo dozed off. He slept fitfully, awakening whenever one of the sentries came by. The night passed uneventfully, and the first streaks of dawn were coloring the eastern horizon bright pink when he rose and saddled the stallion.

Only one other person was up and about. Ben Reardon came to the picket line to saddle his own horse. He made no comment, but the glare he shot Fargo was eloquent testimony to the hatred he harbored. Once mounted, he trotted eastward.

Fargo went in a different direction, due north. A long time had gone by since he last passed through that particular territory, but he seemed to recall there being a small yearlong stream to the north—close enough to save the earl's stock, provided he could find it.

Greenhorns like Hadden never failed to amaze Fargo. They treated the wilderness as if it were their plaything, taking it for granted that whatever they needed would come along just when they needed it. Many a time Fargo had found the remains of those who learned the hard way that wasn't the case.

To survive in the West a person had to be able to wrest from nature those things crucial to survival. Water, food, shelter—they were all there if a person knew where to look for them. If the person didn't, then he or she could starve in the midst of plenty, or die of thirst when an underground spring lay a few short feet under their fingertips.

The West was no place for amateurs, or for high-and-mighty noblemen who thought the sun rose and set just for their benefit.

As soon as the sun climbed the sky the air grew warm and muggy. Fargo pushed his hat back and held the pinto to a brisk walk. He came across fresh buffalo sign, a small herd that had meandered westward. Later he found evidence of a larger herd, but the spoor was a week old.

Several hours went by. By midmorning Fargo figured he had made a mistake and the stream was a lot farther north than he had counted on. He gave the plain a final survey and was on the verge of wheeling the pinto when his keen eyes spotted a unique insect flitting about the tops of the grass.

Ordinary bugs such as flies and crickets were as common as fleas on a mongrel. But the tiny blue insect darting to and fro was unique in that its kind was found only near water. Gossamer wings shimmering, the dragonfly went about its business undisturbed.

Fargo draped a forearm on his saddle horn and waited. Eventually the dragonfly made a beeline to the northwest. Fargo applied his spurs and soon spied a thin ribbon of vegetation, the hallmark of excess moisture.

The stream was even smaller than Fargo remembered, little more than a trickle connecting random shallow pools. He let the Ovaro drink its fill, and while relaxing in the saddle he spied moccasin tracks a few yards away. Suddenly alert, he swung to the ground, and as he did a rifle boomed in the distance and a slug whizzed above the Ovaro.

Instantly Fargo shucked the Sharps and gave the pinto a hard slap on the rump to get it out of there before the rifleman brought it down. He knew the stallion wouldn't go far, and he wanted to be free to concentrate on staying alive.

Crouching, Fargo slid a cartridge into his rifle. A clod of dirt shot up into his face at the same moment that he heard the next shot. Diving into the sparse weeds bordering the pool, he snaked his way to a thin cottonwood and peeked around it.

The rifleman was to the east, in denser growth, and try as he might Fargo couldn't spot him. He lifted his head a bit higher and promptly regretted doing so when a slug tore into the sapling, gouging an inch-deep furrow and nearly taking off his ear.

Rolling to the right, Fargo dug his elbows and knees in and crawled to a willow. The trunk was wider, offering more cover. He cocked the Sharps and set the trigger, then eased into a squat.

The way Fargo saw it, either Ben Reardon had decided to settle accounts or a lone Arapaho was hungry for a scalp. He leaned on the willow, his eyes and ears straining. As the minutes passed and he saw no one, he questioned whether the man was still there.

Then Fargo saw several sunflowers in the middle of a

sunflower patch quiver as if shaken by the wind. Only there was no wind. Taking aim on the very center, he stroked the trigger and felt the stock slap against his shoulder.

One of the sunflower plants was blasted apart, there was a startled yelp, and whoever had been hiding in the patch darted into a stand of young oaks.

Fargo was unable to see the man clearly. He ejected the spent cartridge and inserted another, but by then the shooter had gone to ground.

A test of wills took place. Fargo waited for the shooter to show himself, and the shooter waited for Fargo to do the same. Neither moved from his vantage point. At least Fargo didn't *see* the rifleman move, and he assumed the killer was still hidden there.

With quiet restored, birds resumed chirping and somewhere up the stream a lone frog croaked.

Fargo wasn't lulled into letting down his guard. He constantly checked out from both sides of the willow, but the only living thing he saw was a butterfly. That is, until he saw the eyeball.

He was scouring the undergrowth for the fiftieth time when his gaze drifted past the midsection of an oak tree and a pale knob at the edge of the trunk struck him as so unusual he looked at it again—and saw it blink. Suddenly realizing the truth, he snapped up the Sharps and fired just as the eyeball yanked back. He heard a crash, as of a splintering limb, then the sound of rapid footsteps leading eastward.

Rising, Fargo grabbed the Colt from its holster and gave chase. Ahead a vague figure barreled through the brush. Fargo could distinguish few details, but one was very apparent—the man limped slightly. The fall from the oak had hurt him.

Suddenly the rifleman came to a clear gap and bolted across it instead of going around. It was the moment Fargo had been hoping for. Extending the Colt, he banged off a single shot and was rewarded by seeing the figure pitch headlong to the grass. Rushing forward, Fargo stood over the man, and only then did he realize who it was.

Perplexed, Fargo stared at the angular features of the bodyguard named Moulton, the one he had shared a table with the evening before, and tried to make sense of the attack. Since none of the bodyguards would lift a finger against him without the earl's say-so, the logical conclusion was that Hadden had sent Moulton to kill him.

Why, though? The earl had been acting as friendly as could be, leaving Fargo at a complete loss to explain the attempt on his life. Or had the friendliness all been an act so Fargo wouldn't suspect the earl's real intentions?

A low groan disclosed that Moulton was still alive. Sinking to one knee, Fargo discovered a flesh wound on the man's right temple. He quickly took Moulton's rifle and pistol and threw them aside, then stood and stepped back.

The Englishman groaned louder, moving his limbs sluggishly. He slowly put a hand to his head and his eyes opened.

"It never pays to catch bullets with your skull," Fargo remarked.

Moulton shoved upright and swung around. His right hand swooped under his jacket, then he tensed.

"Lose something?" Fargo asked, wagging an elbow at the rifle and pistol.

"What do you want?" Moulton snapped.

"That's a stupid question coming from someone who just tried to bushwhack me."

"I'll never tell you a thing!"

"I think you will," Fargo said, and taking a swift step he kicked the Britisher full in the chest, flinging Moulton into a patch of clover. "We don't have to do this the hard way," Fargo said. "It's up to you."

"Do you think you can scare me as you did Reardon? I'm not a country bumpkin," Moulton growled. "I was with the king's Dragoon Guards."

The name meant nothing to Fargo, and his expression must have shown as much because the Englishman felt fit to elaborate.

"The Guards are made up of the best fighting men in England," Moulton boasted. "I fought in Africa and India against blighters who make you look as tame as a kitten."

Fargo had moved closer while the bodyguard talked. He still held the Sharps in his left hand and he abruptly slashed the barrel at Moulton's cheek. It connected, drawing blood, causing Moulton to jerk rearward and sprawl onto his back. "This cat has claws," Fargo warned, "and I'll use them if you don't tell me why you tried to kill me."

The bodyguard clammed up.

"I've done nothing to you," Fargo went on. "The best I can figure it, Hadden put you up to this. But I haven't given him any reason to want me dead. Not yet, anyway."

Moulton smoldered with pent-up rage. "Don't play the innocent with me!" he exploded. "You know damn well why this happened, and it has nothing to do with the earl!"

Fargo was genuinely surprised. "If he's not behind it, then who is?"

The bodyguard had pressed his hands flat, seemingly about to sit up. He did rise, but he did so as if shot from a cannon, at the same time hurling twin handfuls of dirt at Fargo's face just as Fargo was staring thoughtfully at the ground, trying to deduce who was to blame for the attempt on his life.

Fargo glanced up and the dirt hit him full in the eyes. He automatically snapped off a shot, but his eyes were already watering and he missed by a hair. A shoulder gouged into his stomach as he thumbed back the hammer, iron arms banded his middle, and he was lifted off his feet and smashed to the earth. The Sharps was jarred from his grasp.

Fingers closed on Fargo's wrist and he felt Moulton trying to pry the Colt loose. Blinking furiously, Fargo tried to clear his blurry vision. He swung a punch that the bodyguard blocked and took one in the gut in return.

"Let go, damn you!" Moulton bellowed, slamming Fargo's gun hand on the ground.

Hooking a knee, Fargo pushed, seeking to throw the Englishman from him. Moulton clung on tenaciously, boxing him across the mouth twice in a row. Pain seared Fargo's head and he tasted blood on his tongue.

The Colt started to slip loose. Fargo redoubled his efforts, throwing himself to the left, sweeping Moulton along with him. They grappled, the bodyguard still clawing at the six-gun. Rolling over and over, they collided with a tree and Fargo was pinned on the bottom. Somehow the Colt ended up between them and he could feel the barrel poking into his ribs. He twisted, heaved, and heard a muffled retort.

Moulton sagged, going slack.

Slowly untangling himself, Skye Fargo rose and looked down at the crimson hole in the chest of the man who had tried to kill him. He would have to get the answer to his question somewhere else. "Damn," he said softly.

Now what was he going to do?

5

Either Ashley Hadden, the Earl of Somerset, was talented enough to be on the stage, or he was truly confused and upset when he heard Skye Fargo's fabricated story about finding Moulton's belongings out on the prairie. "This just can't be!" he declared. "Why would Eric Moulton leave camp without my permission? Where did he think he was going?"

"You'd have to ask him," Fargo hedged. "I just brought back his horse, guns, and hat." The last item had been the only article of Moulton's clothing Fargo hadn't buried, and then only because the bodyguard had stitched his name into the hatband.

The earl examined the headgear, then looked about him at the assembled members of his party. "Mr. Brockton!"

A spindly man pushed through to the front. "Sir?"

"You're in charge of our animals. Why did you let Mr. Moulton take one without my consent?"

"He told me that he did have your permission, sir."

"And you believed him?"

"I had no reason not to. Besides, he was one of your bodyguards, sir, and you pretty much let them come and go as they please. I assumed he was doing something for you."

"You assumed wrong!" Hadden fumed. He stared at Fargo again. "And there was no sign of Moulton himself? Just the things you brought back?"

"There's no trace of your man," Fargo said, which was true enough since no one would ever find the body. He had decided to bury the Englishman and come back with his horse to gauge the reaction of the others and possibly flush out the one responsible for siccing Moulton on him. While still not completely convinced the earl wasn't to blame,

53

there was enough of a doubt for him to hold off on confronting Hadden until he had more proof.

"Could the redskins have gotten hold of him?" the earl asked.

"Anything is possible," Fargo conceded.

"Then we should launch a search, scour the countryside," Hadden proposed with vigor. "We'll turn over every blade of grass until we find him!"

"What about the ladies?" Fargo inquired with a polite nod at the three women standing behind the nobleman. "If the men go traipsing all over creation looking for your bodyguard, who will be here to protect the women if the Indians attack?"

"I'll take half the men," Hadden said.

"Indians have been known to lure travelers from their camps to kill them. The Apaches do it all the time," Fargo said. This, too, was true as far as it went. The Apaches were indeed masters at deception. The Arapahos, however, used more straightforward tactics.

"Are you saying we should forget about Eric? Leave him out there at the mercy of those savages, or perhaps to be eaten by wild beasts?" Hadden shook his head. "Never! He's a fellow Englishman, and we do not desert our own!"

Murmurs of assent broke out among the Britishers.

Fargo hadn't counted on this. If the nobleman and his company went on a hunt in their frame of mind, there would be hell to pay if they ran into the Arapahos. He was mulling over what argument he could use to convince them to change their minds when the matter was taken out of his hands by the timely arrival of Ben Reardon.

The scout charged out of the high grass and reined to a sliding stop. "Your Highness!" he bawled, vaulting from the saddle and nearly tripping over his own feet. "This is your chance! You've got to come, pronto!"

"What are you on about?" Hadden demanded irritably.

"That big bull you wanted," Reardon said. "I finally found you one."

"You did?" Hadden asked in surprise.

"That's right. And it's a dandy." Reardon motioned to the southeast. "But you'd better light a shuck or it's liable to have wandered off before you get there."

"How big is it?" the earl pressed him, his face lit with excitement.

"Biggest damn buffalo I ever laid eyes on," Reardon said. "Must stand six and a half feet high at the shoulders and have a horn spread of four feet."

Fargo couldn't suppress a smile. He had his doubts the scout had seen one so huge. The average height was six feet, the average horn spread about half that. From time to time giant bulls were spotted, but they didn't last long. Once word spread, every warrior from Canada to Mexico was out after its hide.

Fargo suspected that once Reardon guided the earl to the spot where the bull supposedly had been, the animal would have disappeared. He believed Reardon had made the claim so he wouldn't be fired.

And it was obvious that Ashley Hadden was going to go. The nobleman positively glowed with the thrill of the impending hunt. "At last!" he declared. "I'll bag my trophy!" In the span of moments, he had forgotten all about his missing bodyguard, but he wasn't let off the hook that easily.

"Sir, what about Moulton?" Oakley asked.

The reminder jarred the earl. He had a choice to make: to decide between personal glory or the welfare of one of his own, and the decision he reached was damning. "Right. We can't forget about him, can we?" He made a show of scratching his chin, as if thinking. "Here's what we'll do. I'll take ten men and go with Reardon to check on his buffalo, while you, Mr. Oakley, will take six men and lead our remaining horses to the stream Mr. Fargo discovered. Along the way, look for signs of Mr. Moulton."

Fargo had done some fast mental calculations. "Do that and there will be only two men left behind to guard the women."

"What?" Hadden turned down his mouth. "Your concern for the fairer sex is commendable, Mr. Fargo. To put you at ease, I'll leave two more men in camp. Will that do?"

"Not if the Arapahos stage a raid."

"They didn't attack this morning as you asserted they would. What makes you think they'll try before sunset?"

"No one can predict when they'll strike, if ever," Fargo said.

"I thought as much," Hadden said stiffly. He clapped his hands to draw attention. "All right, people. You heard my instructions. Let's get cracking."

The staff moved to obey, but there was a noticeable lack of enthusiasm in their actions. Oakley and several other men were clearly displeased, yet they went about their jobs without complaint.

Fargo stayed where he was, observing. He still didn't understand why the English group let themselves be lorded over by the likes of Ashley Hadden. But it wasn't his place to object, so he said nothing.

Kendra Hadden came toward him. "I wanted to thank you for speaking in our behalf. When my husband is in one of his hunting moods, he doesn't always think straight."

"I didn't think you were talking to me anymore," Fargo said bluntly.

"I'll confess I was somewhat unnerved by your manners," the countess said. "For a while I regarded you as an uncouth lout and wanted nothing to do with you. But now Flora tells me I'm making a mistake, that deep down you're a decent person."

"How would she know?" Fargo asked with a devilish grin.

Kendra laughed, then put a hand to her mouth as if she had committed a terrible breach of etiquette.

"It won't hurt you to crack a smile now and then," Fargo told her.

"You don't understand."

"I might surprise you," Fargo said, noticing how rosy her lips were in the sunlight. He inhaled the tantalizing scent of her perfume and felt a familiar hunger.

Kendra looked at him, a silent appeal in the depths of her lovely eyes. She lightly grasped his fingers. "Please. I don't know what Flora has told you, but don't make an issue of it."

"You'd rather go on being miserable?"

"It's my life."

Fargo was inclined to debate the point, but Elizabeth Hadden just then called from the main tent.

"Countess! Time for our tea!"

"I must go," Kendra said sadly.

"We'll talk again," Fargo told her. Just that brief contact had set his blood to racing, and as he watched her walk off, admiring her lustrous hair, the flare of her hips, and the enticing sway of her lithe legs as her dress swished against them, he felt his loins twitch. Every so often a man came across a woman who aroused him to a fever pitch with her very presence, and Kendra Hadden had that effect on him. He couldn't get her out of his system, even though the way things stood he was wasting his time.

A minute later Reardon rode up. "The earl wants you to tag along with us."

"What about Oakley's bunch?"

"Hell, I don't know. I reckon the earl doesn't care much one way or the other. Just point them in the right direction and send them on their way."

Fargo walked to where the wounded bodyguard and six others were gathering the first group of horses to be taken to water. "I'm not going with you," he announced.

"We've already been told," the dapper Oakley responded with a sharp glance at the earl, who was organizing his own group a dozen yards off. "But not to worry. I've a fair sense of direction. Tell me how to get there and we'll make it back, I guarantee."

Fargo did, and Oakley thanked him. "Be on the lookout for those Arapahos," Fargo went on. "Always have your rifles ready, and never let down your guard. With luck, they'll let you alone and you'll make it back before sunset."

"By rights we should simply move the whole camp," Oakley said.

"Why don't you mention that to the earl?"

"And be chewed out for overstepping my station?"

"I'll try talking some sense into him," Fargo offered. He led the Ovaro over and was greeted with a clap on the shoulder.

"You're ready! Fine!" Hadden exclaimed, so thrilled he could hardly contain himself. "We're almost saddled."

Fargo looked at the horses, hanging their heads with fatigue. "These animals aren't in any better shape than the rest. You should take them all to the stream. Make it easy on yourself and move the camp before they give out on you."

"And pass up this chance to add another trophy beast to my collection?" The earl shook his head. "Not on your life. Reardon informed me the bull is less than two miles away. It won't strain the horses to go a while longer without a drink."

Fargo mounted without saying another word and fell in behind the rest as the scout led them at a gallop out across the prairie. He looked back once and saw the countess watching. She looked so lonely standing there by herself—so neglected. The earl had to be half-loco, Fargo reflected, to ignore a beautiful woman like that just to go after big game. The countess waved, so Fargo did likewise.

True to Reardon's word, within two miles a buffalo herd came into sight, thousands upon thousands of the great, shaggy brutes dotting the landscape for as far as the eye could see, all grazing contentedly.

The scout chose a low knoll to spy on them. Taking a telescope from his saddlebags, he climbed with the earl to the top. The others stayed on their horses, but not Fargo. He was curious about the monster bull.

"See him, Your Highness?" Reardon was whispering as Fargo lowered onto his stomach beside them. "About five hundred yards out, near a wallow?"

Hadden fiddled with the telescope, then gasped. "I say! He's magnificent! Everything you've claimed, and more!" After watching for a while, he handed the spyglass to Fargo. "Take a look and see if you agree."

It would have been impossible not to. A thrill rippled down Fargo's spine when he set eyes on the brute. It was enormous, every inch as big as Reardon had estimated. At the moment the bull was urinating in a dry wallow, and once done, it rolled vigorously back and forth, caking itself with mud to ward off annoying insects.

"What's your opinion?" Hadden asked eagerly. "Have you ever seen one bigger?"

"Can't say that I have," Fargo confessed.

"I can see the head now, hanging above my hearth." The earl scuttled backward until he was below the crest, then rose. "Come on, you two. Let's dash out there and put an end to him before he takes it into his head to go elsewhere."

"Not so fast," Reardon said. "These mangy critters aren't

like those water buffalo in Africa that you were telling me about the other day. You go rushing on out there and you're liable to cause a stampede."

"He'll run?"

"The whole herd will run," Reardon amended. "Spook one buffalo and you spook them all. There must be fifty or sixty between us and him, so if you set them off, you'll never get a clear shot."

"What do you suggest I do?"

"Wait for him to come closer."

"Like hell I will. He might go in the other direction. Then where would I be?" The earl gazed at Fargo. "How would you go about it?"

"Indian fashion. Since we don't have any coyote hides, our horses will have to do."

"Show me."

Fargo explained as he descended. "Coyotes can move freely among a herd when it's spread out, so sometimes Indians cover themselves with coyote skins and crawl on their hands and knees right up to the buffalo they want to kill. A few arrows into its hide, and they have their meat." He paused. "At other times they ride right in, hanging on to the sides of their horses. Unless the buffalo catch a whiff of man-scent, they can do the same thing."

"And if the herd does catch their scent?"

"They ride like hell." Fargo climbed onto the Ovaro and demonstrated the Sioux technique he had learned during the time he lived with the tribe. Looping an elbow over the pinto's neck, he slid onto its side while at the same time hooking an ankle on its back. The trick was best done bareback, and Fargo had to be careful not to snag his buckskins on his saddle as he moved down, then back up. "Think you can do it?"

"Are you jesting?" Hadden mounted his English thoroughbred and flawlessly did as Fargo had done, the feat made easier by his smaller, smoother English saddle. "I could to this in my sleep," he bragged. "Hand me my new rifle, Heath."

One of the men held out a gleaming Spencer.

Fargo was not obligated to say anything. He could have sat there and let the nobleman ride into the herd bearing a rifle notorious for failing to drop anything bigger than a white-tailed deer. But he commented, "I'd use another gun. The Spencer isn't powerful enough to drop that bull with one shot."

"So? The magazine holds seven bullets. If the first one doesn't do the job, I'll keep firing."

"Be my guest," Fargo said, folding his arms. He had spoken his piece. No one could ever say he let the nobleman ride to his death so the countess would be available.

The earl lifted his reins and glanced at the scout. "Why are you standing there like a bump on a log, Mr. Reardon? Kindly mount and join me."

"Not me. I'm not going out into that herd. If they stampede I might be killed."

"Yes, you," Hadden insisted. "I agreed to pay you top wages in return for your assistance in bagging my trophy. So you will stay with me every step of the way and whisper whatever advice is needed as we go along."

Reardon reluctantly stepped into the stirrups. "I don't like this, mister, but I'll uphold my end of our bargain."

"Money can be terribly persuasive," the earl said caustically. Taking the lead, he rode to the end of the knoll, then slipped onto the side of his horse. The scout did the same and they moved on, side by side.

Fargo slid to the ground and dashed to the top again. Crouching, he observed their progress, paying particular attention to the buffalo they passed. At the edge of the herd stood a small bull that looked up from eating, grunted, and shook its hairy head. It studied the two horses a bit, then resumed feeding.

Ashley Hadden was on the right, Ben Reardon on the left. They were on opposite sides of their mounts, within inches of each other. Reardon was talking quietly as they went along, guiding the nobleman.

Only one of the buffalo showed any agitation, a cow with its calf that stamped her front hooves and tossed her horns as if about to charge. She raised her head high, sniffed loudly several times, then moved off, prodding the calf ahead of her.

The huge bull was still rolling in the wallow, and by now mud caked its hump, back, and sides. Suddenly rising, he shook himself and walked into the grass. The horses caught his eye immediately, and for the longest while he stared at them, perhaps debating in his brutish way whether they posed a threat. Apparently convinced they were harmless, he bowed his great head to eat.

Fargo began to think the pair would make it. They covered a hundred yards without mishap and were passing a cluster of cows when the nobleman's thoroughbred abruptly snorted and shied. Fargo could see Hadden trying to bring the nervous horse under control by tugging on the reins. The thoroughbred jerked its head, fighting every step of the way.

Some of the cows had glanced up and were watching with interest.

Fargo wondered why the thoroughbred was acting up. It shied farther from the cows and kicked its front legs, almost dislodging the earl. More and more buffalo were watching, and several bulls had begun moving closer.

Ben Reardon angled his horse toward the thoroughbred to try and help, but the English horse wouldn't allow him to get close enough to grab hold.

Fargo had a hunch that proved to be correct when the thoroughbred veered sharply away from an approaching bull. Unlike an Indian mount or the scout's dun, the earl's horse wasn't accustomed to being so close to the big beasts. Its nerves were frayed, and now it wanted out of the herd.

The commotion had caused all the buffalo within sight of the horse to stop what they were doing and stare.

Fargo knew that Hadden and Reardon were in serious trouble. The slightest mistake might provoke a charge. Or worse, a stampede. He couldn't see their expressions, but he had the impression the earl was in a rage and the scout was attempting to calm him down. Meanwhile, the thoroughbred danced back and forth in a small circle, its head bobbing.

Fargo heard footsteps and twisted to see the bodyguard named Heath coming toward him. He motioned for the man to keep low.

"What's happening, mate?" Heath asked.

"They're in a tight fix."

Heath looked and tensed. "We should ride out and protect his nibs," he declared.

"You do and you'll only make it worse," Fargo said. "Those buffalo are getting wound up to either fight or flee."

A loud whinny carried to their ears. One of the bulls stood fifteen yards from the thoroughbred, which had reared and was swinging its hoofs in the air. When the horse came down, the impact jarred Ashley Hadden loose and he fell onto his side. He started to rise but a word from Reardon made him go prone.

The foremost bull slowly advanced, head low, horns glinting wickedly in the sunlight.

"Sweet Jesus!" Heath exclaimed, turning. "We've got to do something!"

"No!" Fargo said, grabbing the man's arm.

Once more the thoroughbred's whinny drew their gaze. The horse had wheeled and headed back but found its path barred by another bull. Rather than swing around the irritable brute, the horse stubbornly stood its ground, tossing its mane and pounding the ground.

In the meantime Reardon had maneuvered his mount alongside the nobleman and Hadden was slowly rising, his hand reaching for the saddle horn. Their intent was plain. Once Hadden grabbed hold, he could slip a foot into a stirrup and cling to the side of the horse as Reardon brought them to safety.

The plan might have worked had the thoroughbred not chosen that moment to close in on the bull and rear again in an effort to drive the bull off. It had the opposite effect. Bellowing, the bull leveled its horns and charged. Fifteen hundred pounds of solid muscle and bone rammed into the thoroughbred's belly, bowling the horse over. The thoroughbred squealed in fright as it went down, a squeal that changed to a wavering neigh of agony the next moment as a curved horn tore through its hide and flesh and ripped its stomach wide open.

Then everything seemed to happen at once.

Ashley Hadden straightened to swing onto the dun just as another bull charged it and the dun broke into a run to escape. The earl was flung to the ground in front of the bull and frantically scrambled out of the way.

Heath yanked loose from Fargo and raced down the slope, shouting to the others that the earl was in danger. They promptly goaded their horses into a gallop, speeding to the nobleman's rescue.

Skye Fargo cursed and saw his worst nightmare come to life. The whole herd lumbered into motion, erupting in a thundering stampede, bulls, cows, and calves forming into a roiling mass that swept pell-mell to the northwest.

Directly toward the knoll.

6

The destructive might of a buffalo stampede had to be seen to be believed. Swept along in a mindless frenzy, a herd crushed everything in its path, trampling brush and trees and even other creatures under thousands of flying hooves. It stopped for nothing short of total exhaustion and swerved aside for few obstacles. Any person caught in its path was reduced to a gory pulp in seconds.

Skye Fargo knew all this, which is why he whirled and bolted, flying down the knoll and vaulting into the saddle from a dead run. Instantly the Ovaro lit out and Fargo slanted slightly to the left so he could mark the herd's progress. He saw Heath and the other Englishmen rein up, saw them unlimber their rifles and fire shots into the herd in a futile bid to check the onrushing horde.

Then the leading ranks reached the Britishers and both men and horses disappeared under a river of shaggy humps and choking clouds of dust. There were screams and whinnies and several shots, and finally just the din of rumbling thunder.

Fargo applied his spurs, lashed his reins. The stallion flowed over the ground, equally aware of the certain death closing in on their heels. Looking back, Fargo saw a wide onrushing line of broad heads, shaggy manes, and scraggly beards. The line extended for scores of yards in either direction, too far for him to consider cutting to either side in order to swing around the herd. His only hope lay in flight.

Fargo faced forward and devoted all his attention to the lay of the land. A single rut or prairie-dog hole could spell disaster. If the Ovaro went down, the herd would be on them before he could get the pinto on its feet. He tried to recall whether they had passed any prairie-dog towns on their way from camp, and couldn't.

Camp! The thought knit Fargo's gut into a tight ball. The herd was heading right for the encampment! Unless he could pull ahead, there would be little warning for those left there. The women wouldn't stand a prayer.

Bending forward, Fargo urged the stallion on. Over short distances a buffalo and a horse were evenly matched, but on long stretches the greater stamina of the horse always won out. He was counting on that fact to enable him to reach the camp a minute or so ahead of the herd.

A quarter of a mile opened between them. Then half a mile. Fargo repeatedly glanced around in hope the herd would stop, and although the brutes did slow they showed no signs of tiring. A billowing cloud enveloped all but the leaders and blotted out a goodly portion of the sky.

Ahead, Fargo spied something else spiraling skyward— the column of smoke from the campfire. He had gained several hundred yards on the buffalo, far too few to avert tragedy unless he could somehow forewarn Kendra and the rest.

A mile was covered and Fargo gained a few hundred more yards. Soon he spotted figures moving about, and drawing his Colt, he banged off four spaced shots. That got their attention, but they stood there staring beyond him, trying to figure out what was creating the dust cloud. "Run!" Fargo shouted, waving his arm. "Get the hell out of there!"

The four men, Flora Livingstone, and Elizabeth Hadden were converging at the edge of the camp. Not a one of them made a move toward the picket line.

"Ride for your lives!" Fargo bellowed as he approached. "Stampede!"

Still the Britishers stood there, gawking. Fargo reined up, jabbed a hand at the dust cloud, and barked, "Those are buffalo! Unless you want to die, mount up and ride!"

"But Skye," Flora said fearfully, "we can't! Oakley took the horses with him, remember?"

Fargo recoiled as if slapped. In all the excitement he had forgotten about the stock being taken to the stream. Furious, he glanced at the empty picket rope, then at the oncoming beasts, then at the anxious, upturned faces of those doomed by a nobleman's pigheaded stupidity to end their lives in the grisliest manner conceivable. Or were they?

Fargo pointed at the wagons and shouted at the men. "Flip them over, tongue to tongue, to make a barricade! *Move!*" He looked at Flora and Elizabeth. "The two of you get behind the wagons and dig in."

"I will not," Elizabeth Hadden said. "I demand to know where my brother is. He'll know how to properly handle this situation."

There was no time to spend in senseless arguing. Fargo moved the Ovaro closer, leaned down, and slapped the earl's sister, hard. She raised a hand to her red cheek and stood dumbfounded, her lips quivering, her eyes brimming with tears. "Now do as I told you!" Fargo bellowed, giving her a shove.

Flora grabbed Elizabeth's arm and pulled the flustered woman toward the vans. "We've got to hurry!" A look of horror came over her and she paused, stabbing an arm to the west. "Oh, my God! Kendra!"

"What about her?"

"She went for a stroll!"

"Get to the wagons!" Fargo ordered, jabbing his spurs into the pinto's flanks. He raced out of the camp and spotted a solitary figure in the distance. The countess had gone half a mile, maybe more. Fargo pulled his Colt and fired again, desperately trying to get her attention.

Kendra stopped and turned.

From the southeast came the buffalo, their coats flecked with foamy sweat. The force of the stampede had slackened, but not enough. Fargo shifted and watched as the front line of bobbing beasts overran the hollow, raising a blanket of dust. He thought the horde parted to swerve around the wagons, but he couldn't be sure. Then he heard wood splinter and a piercing scream. Guns boomed.

Working the reins, his legs pumping against the pinto's slick sides, Fargo bore down on the Countess of Somerset. Unless he swung her up behind his saddle and outran the herd, she would be torn to ribbons. The gap between them shrank until he could see her worried features. She was running toward him, the hem of her dress held high to allow more freedom of movement, and despite the perilous situation Fargo couldn't take his eyes off her sleek legs and satiny thighs.

"What is it?" Kendra called. "What is happening?"

Fargo shook himself and answered, "Buffalo stampede! Hold out your arm!"

Kendra understood and stopped, her left arm aloft, her body coiled to absorb the shock of being wrenched off her feet.

"Smart girl," Fargo said under his breath. Then he was almost abreast of her and bending to the left, his own arm outstretched for the grab. She took a hop and he had her, holding her supple form close as he straightened and lifted her onto the back of the Ovaro. Her arms clasped around his waist and warm breath fluttered in his ear.

"What about the others? Flora?"

"I don't know," Fargo responded. He couldn't help but notice that she didn't ask about Ashley, and he smiled.

By this time the buffalo had swept well beyond the hollow. Fargo could tell the Ovaro was tiring rapidly, and when a horse was tired it made mistakes. He stayed alert for holes or depressions, conscious of the feel of Kendra's chest against his back, of the friction of her breasts on his buckskin.

For another three-quarters of a mile the stampede continued. Then, at long last, Fargo noted a change in the rhythm of the pounding hooves. He looked and discovered the buffalo were finally slowing. In less than a minute the great beasts had stopped and were milling about, puffing and blowing from their exertion.

Fargo brought the stallion to a halt. The Ovaro was winded, in need of a breather, and he commented as much to the countess, adding, "Let's climb down and walk a spell. We'll ride on back as soon as my horse is cooled off."

Kendra Hadden slid gracefully off, seemingly unaware her dress hiked high on her creamy legs. She ran her hand through her golden locks while staring thoughtfully at the buffalo. "You saved my life," she said softly.

"Couldn't let that pretty dress of yours get ruined." Fargo tried to make light of the incident, but she didn't smile.

Taking the reins, he headed to the south in order to circle around the exhausted herd.

"Ashley would never have done as much for me," Kendra said, falling into step beside him. "Where is he, by the way?"

"Last I saw, a bull was using his backside for target practice."

"Oh my. Was he hurt?"

"I couldn't stick around to find out or I'd be worm food."

"Has anyone every told you that you have a marvelous way with words?"

"No."

"Or about the effect you have on women?" Kendra went on. "When I'm around you, I feel so at ease, so open. I say things I know I shouldn't, things I would never say to anyone else. And the wonder of it is that I hardly know you!"

"Maybe you're just lonely and you have no one else you can talk to."

The countess opened her mouth to respond but changed her mind and was quiet for a while. "Are you always so brutally frank?" she asked at length.

"Does that bother you?"

"No. Yes. I don't know." Kendra fiddled with a tiny bow on her blouse. "It's just that I'm not accustomed to being treated as if I were—"

"—a normal person?" Fargo finished for her.

Kendra nodded and grinned. "Everyone else treats me as if I can walk on water, except Elizabeth, of course, who despises the very air I breathe."

"I've noticed she doesn't think too highly of you."

"There's an understatement. If she could murder me and get away with it, I swear she would."

"Quite a family you married into," Fargo said.

"I didn't have any choice."

"So I've heard."

The countess stopped and turned to face him. "I don't like your tone. You're not in a position to judge me because you know nothing of my background, or of England. Things are done differently over there. Yes, I made a mistake marrying Ashley, and now I'm stuck with him."

"You deserve better. You deserve to be happy."

"I've come to the conclusion it isn't our lot in life to know true happiness. The best we can hope for is that our suffering will be kept to a minimum." She waved a hand as if dismissing the subject. "Enough about me. What would make you happy, Skye Fargo? What do you want more than anything else in this world?"

"To kiss you."

Kendra Hadden blinked, then laughed. "Really. You just don't come right out and tell a woman something like that."

"Why not?" Fargo responded, letting the reins drop and stepping in front of her so they were nose to nose. "I was serious."

A crimson tinge streaked Kendra's cheeks. "I must insist that you behave yourself."

"Why, when you know that you want me to do it?"

"I do not!"

"Care to put your money where your mouth is?" Fargo asked, and before she could reply, he put an arm around her slender waist and pulled her close. Her eyes flared and she raised a hand to punch him. Ignoring both, he slowly touched his lips to hers and felt her stiffen against him. He kissed her lightly, delicately, savoring the sensation. When he lifted his head, she had not moved.

"You are a horrible brute!"

Fargo kissed her again, harder this time, mashing his mouth into hers while running his hand up her spine. She put both hands on his shoulders as if to shove him away but instead held fast, her lips parting to admit his probing tongue. The sweet taste of her was intoxicating, and Fargo let the kiss linger on and on.

Kendra panted when they broke for air. "I must insist that you try to behave like a gentleman," she said, but her eyes told another story.

For the third time Fargo bent his lips to hers, and this time she inhaled his tongue while grinding against him with passionate abandon. He cupped her buttocks, heard her groan hungrily low in her throat. Her hot palms pressed on his neck, his face. Their tongues tangled together, and he could feel her warm breath on his face.

The kiss lasted longer than any so far. On drawing back, Fargo was surprised to see moisture brimming in her eyes.

She bowed her forehead to his shoulder and squeezed his arms. "Are you all right?" he asked.

"My head is swimming."

Fargo pecked her on the hair and held her close. "Still figure I'm a brute?"

"For forcing me to admit the truth, yes," Kendra said. "Oh, Skye! What am I going to do?" Suddenly she trembled and erupted in tears, clinging to him in desperation.

No words were necessary. Fargo held her for the longest while, until she had cried herself out and sagged limply in his arms. He kept her from falling, waiting for her to recover. Looking down, he saw that her hair had fallen away from the back of her neck, revealing an ugly dark circle as big as his fist. "Where did you get that bruise?" he inquired.

The countess sniffed and straightened. "I bumped myself," she said, nervously smoothing her dress.

"Like hell you did. It was the earl, wasn't it? How many more do you have?"

Kendra averted her face and pleaded in a whisper, "Please. Just take me back. This has all been too much for me. I need some time to think, to sort out what I should do."

Reluctantly, Fargo complied. After walking a short distance to rest the pinto, he boosted Kendra into the saddle and climbed up behind her. The buffalo had spread out to graze, forcing him to swing farther south than he'd anticipated. As a result, half an hour went by before he spotted the camp, or what was left of it.

The tents were either in tattered ruins or gone, the poles lying in shattered bits. Smashed personal effects were scattered everywhere. Torn clothes littered the ground. One of the wagons was a broken wreck, the sides and roof caved in, the tongue split in half, the wheels busted beyond repair. The other van had a crack in the side but was otherwise undamaged.

Fargo was more concerned about the people. He saw a body partially covered with a ripped blanket near the wagons. Close by stood three Englishmen, one having his arm tended, another with blood trickling from a scalp wound. Of Flora and Elizabeth he saw neither hide nor hair, and he was becoming worried for Flora's safety when she rose up behind the second wagon and spied them.

"Countess! You're safe!"

They came on the run, all except Elizabeth Hadden who stood next to the intact van and scowled in displeasure at seeing Kendra and Fargo alive.

"We were worried sick about you," Flora said as she helped the countess down. "I wanted to go find you but Elizabeth wouldn't let me."

Fargo slid onto his saddle and sat with arms folded while Flora and the men fell all over themselves making Kendra comfortable. The countess was too depressed to do more than mumble replies and accept a cup of water from a salvaged canteen with a bleak nod of her pale face.

Flora came over to the Ovaro. "The poor dear," she said quietly. "This ordeal has shaken her up badly. I've never seen her like this."

Fargo saw no reason to tell Flora the truth. "No sign of the earl or anyone else?" he wondered aloud, gazing to the southeast.

"Not yet. Maybe you should go have a look. We'll start picking up the pieces." Flora put a hand on his boot. "I'll look after Kendra personally."

"I won't be long," Fargo promised, trotting off. There was no need to take his bearings by the sun; for scores of yards on either side the grass had been flayed from the ground and the earth pockmarked with countless hoofprints, forming a dirt track that led him straight toward the knoll.

Fargo spotted the three men before they spotted him. One limped and another assisted the third, who couldn't put weight on his left leg. They were too far off for him to identify, but as he drew near he hoped that none of them was the Earl of Somerset, for Kendra's sake. But fate was not going to let her off the hook so easily.

The limping man was Ben Reardon. He had his rifle slanted over his shoulder and looked as miserable as it was possible for a human being to look. He was covered with dust and grime, his hat gone, his shirt torn.

The man who couldn't walk was one of the bodyguards.

His right pant leg was split, and a fragment of bone jutted through the skin.

None other than Ashley Hadden was supporting him under an arm. The nobleman's clothes were rumpled, but otherwise he had come through the stampede unharmed. "Fargo!" he declared, stopping. "Thank goodness you were able to get away in time! What about the camp?"

"Gone."

"My word! And my sister?" the earl asked, so worried he forgot himself and almost let go of the injured bodyguard.

"She's safe," Fargo reported, adding pointedly, "So is your wife."

"That's nice to hear," Hadden said, his attitude showing it was anything but. "Well, step down and give Williams here a hand back. I'll be taking your horse."

"No."

Now Hadden did release the bodyguard, his right hand drifting toward the flap of his jacket. "I'm not making a request, my good fellow. I need to hurry, so you will be so kind as to lend me your pinto without delay."

"No," Fargo repeated, ready to draw if pushed, when he suddenly realized he had made a boneheaded blunder. Any frontiersman worthy of the handle knew to reload after expending all the cartridges in a gun, but he had neglected to do just that after the stampede. His Colt was empty.

Ben Reardon took a step to one side and declared, "Go ahead and pull your iron on him, Your Highness. You saw how quick he was when I braced him. I'd love to see Fargo put windows in your skull."

The reminder caused Hadden to hesitate.

"Yes, sir," Reardon continued with a sneer, "I'll even do the planting myself just so I can spit on your grave."

The insult gave the earl someone else to focus his spite on. "One more word out of you and you're fired."

"Think I give a damn?" Reardon said. "In case you haven't figured it out yet, I'm quitting. You nearly got me killed back there because you're too pigheaded to listen to good advice. Thanks to you, I lost my horse, my saddle, my bedroll—practically everything I own in this world."

"You can't desert us now."

"This is a free country, mister. I can do what I please."

Reardon limped onward, then got off a parting verbal shot over his shoulder. "I am sick to death of watching you grow callouses on your hands from patting yourself on the back. If I hadn't needed the money so bad, I would have left you to get yourself killed weeks ago." Pausing, he looked at Fargo. "And while I'm at it, I might as well apologize for going for my hardware when you hit me. You had every right, me calling you a liar and all. It was the whiskey made me do it." Squaring his shoulders, he marched away.

Fargo was taken aback by the scout's honesty. He turned the Ovaro, his gaze locked on Ashley Hadden. "You still want to try and take my horse?"

The earl turned the air blue with a string of curse words directed at no one in particular. Lightning danced on his brow as he tramped off without another thought for the bodyguard.

Fargo looked at the man, then bent low and held out his left hand. "The sooner we set that bone, the better you'll feel."

Williams stared at the departing nobleman. "I don't know if I should. Mr. Hadden might not appreciate it."

Once again, Fargo was amazed by the way the English kowtowed to their royalty. "Would you rather lose that leg? That's what will happen if the wound gets infected. The sawbones will have to cut it off with a hacksaw."

The young bodyguard trembled and swallowed. "I see your point. If I'm released when we return to England, so be it." He hopped close so Fargo could hoist him onto the stallion. "I'm in your debt, sir."

Fargo rode toward the encampment. Hadden glared at him, but Fargo paid the man no mind. He did touch his hat as he passed Reardon, who answered with a lopsided grin. Once he was well ahead, he drew his Colt and quickly reloaded. Behind him, the bodyguard whistled.

"You took a big chance, calling the earl's bluff like you did," Williams commented.

"Tell me something I don't know."

The women had found a coffeepot and were boiling water when Fargo arrived. In his absence the three Britishers had set the intact van on its wheels and were now roaming the camp collecting items worth saving.

Fargo helped Williams sit down by the fire, then stood aside so Flora could fuss over him. There was no sign yet of Oakley, Revis, and the other men who had taken the horses to the stream, and Fargo knew there wouldn't be for hours. He stared out over the wreckage, troubled by a premonition that—despite all that had already happened—the worst was yet to come.

And his premonitions were seldom wrong.

7

It was a quiet, grim group that got together early the next morning to talk over their next move. Of the original twenty-one members of the earl's party, nine had now died and three were wounded. The doctor, Revis, had his hands full once he returned from watering the stock; much of his time was spent resetting Williams's badly shattered leg.

Skye Fargo had lent a hand. He'd helped tend enough broken limbs to know just what to do. In addition, he was the only one who could do what had to be done without being squeamish or becoming outright ill.

Now Fargo stood apart from the huddled Britishers, sipping from a tin cup brimming with hot black coffee. He gazed toward the wagon, where Ben Reardon sat in a funk. The scout had wanted to leave at dawn, but the earl had refused to give him a horse—even though there were thirty animals left, more than enough to meet the earl's needs. A loud cough turned Fargo's attention back to the meeting.

"While the loss of our fellows is to be deeply regretted," Ashley Hadden declared, "we all knew the risks when we came on this expedition. As for those of you who were hurt, rest assured you will be well rewarded for your suffering with a large bonus once we're back in England." He stopped and scanned them as if expecting to be thanked for his generosity, but all he received were stony stares.

The physician finally broke the awkward silence. "Speaking of the injured, sir, how soon will we get them to Kansas City? Williams is in need of bed rest and more thorough medical attention than I can give him out here."

The earl scrunched up his nose. "We are not leaving for Kansas City anytime soon. Not while I have yet to accomplish that which I came halfway around the world to do."

Revis half-rose in anger, then sat back down. "Am I to understand you intend to go on hunting?"

"I do."

Whispers broke out. Fargo saw the earl's sister glare like a tigress at bay. Kendra, however, covered her face with a hand and bowed her head.

"Surely you will reconsider, sir," Revis said. "The lives of those who work for you are more important than having a new trophy to mount on your wall."

"Don't ever presume to tell me my priorities," Hadden snapped. "I have talked to Williams and the others and they assure me they are doing fine. Are they wrong? Do you think they are in any immediate danger?"

"No, sir. I'm simply advising you that Williams needs better care if he is to avoid infection."

"A little while longer shouldn't make a difference." Hadden pointed to the northwest. "The herd that destroyed our camp is lingering a few miles off. In a day or two I will have located my bull and brought him down. Surely you can watch over Williams that long?"

"I can try."

Fargo could stand to stay quiet no longer. Once again, the earl was having his own way despite the hardship to the others. Lowering his coffee cup, Fargo said, "Leaving for Kansas City while you still can isn't a bad idea."

"I do not recall asking for your opinion," Hadden said.

"I'm giving it anyway," Fargo said. "Look around you, Hadden. You're out of food, low on water. You have only one wagon left. Most of your supplies are gone, and you've lost all your clothes except those on your back. Reaching Missouri won't be easy."

"We'll manage," Hadden said defiantly, dismissing Fargo with a toss of his head.

"Tell that to the ones who lost their lives in the stampede."

Kendra Hadden stood. "I agree with the doctor and Mr. Fargo, Ashley. By staying we risk undue peril. Most of us should start on back while you remain with a few men and finish your hunt."

Fargo expected an argument, but to his surprise the earl smiled and nodded toward him.

"I'll agree, dearest love, only if you employ your ample charms to persuade Mr. Fargo to help me. With his assistance I feel confident of success."

Kendra had a wary look in her eyes when she replied, "I'm sure I can have no influence on him. As you no doubt have noticed, Mr. Fargo is very much his own man. He does as he pleases."

"You underestimate yourself," Hadden said, moving over to drape an arm across her shoulders. He bared his teeth in a smile that gave his face a wolfish aspect. "Why don't you ask him and see what he says?"

Fargo sensed there was more going on than was apparent, although he had no idea what it was. He suspected the nobleman was making an issue of it in front of everyone else to embarrass Kendra. She was clearly troubled, so in her defense he took a stride and declared, "I'll help you, Hadden, but just so the wounded can head out for Kansas City."

"You will?" the earl asked gleefully. "How noble of you." He gazed on his party. "Very well. You've all heard. Tomorrow you will leave. Revis, the wounded will be placed in the wagon under you care. Are there any questions?"

"I have one," intruded a new voice, and Ben Reardon walked up. "What about me?"

"You've made your bed. Now lie in it," Hadden said bitterly.

"But you can't just leave me out here afoot to fend for myself!" Reardon protested. "Don't you have any human decency? You have to take me back to Kansas City."

Hadden laughed. "Decency? What a strange word coming from you. Aren't you the same man who, until two days ago, spent his every waking minute with a whiskey bottle glued to his lips?"

Fargo was taking another swallow, but the coffee abruptly tasted bitter in his mouth and he upended the cup onto the ground. "Reardon goes back with the rest,'" he said.

"Are you presuming to tell me how to manage my own expedition?" the earl asked with annoyance.

"Do you want that bull or not?"

Hadden nodded. "So that's the way it is. As you wish. Mr. Reardon can ride on top of the van."

"No, you'll give him a horse."

"Don't overstep yourself. I can only be pushed so far."

Fargo gave the cup to Flora. "One other thing. It would help if your people stocked up on jerky before they go. Reardon and I will kill a buffalo and show them how to smoke strips of meat to preserve it. By tomorrow there will be enough to last a week or more." He motioned to the scout and walked off without waiting for a reply.

Reardon fell into step and said out of the corner of his mouth, "Damn! You should see his face! The bastard looks as if somebody shoved a corncob up his ass." He chuckled. "About time he was taken down a notch."

"Before I'm done he'll be taken down a few more," Fargo vowed. He led the way to his bedroll and saddle and then carried both to the Ovaro.

"I'm obliged for what you've done," Reardon commented as he moved along the picket rope to make his pick. "If I can ever repay the favor, just let me know."

Fargo quickly saddled up and mounted. He was checking the Sharps when the scout came alongside him.

"I'd like to get my hands on the idiot who makes these damn puny saddles," Reardon groused. "They aren't fit for a grown man to use." He smacked his in annoyance. "Look at this! No horn, no fork, no cantle—hell, no damn tree at all. A man might as well go bareback."

Flora Livingstone waved as they rode out, and Fargo caught Kendra watching him on the sly so her husband wouldn't notice. He waved back, then brought the pinto to a canter.

"I sure am glad to get away from the earl for a spell," Reardon mentioned. "It's all I can do to not put a bullet in his brain. That man riles me just by being alive."

"He does have a knack," Fargo agreed.

Reardon sighed. "This has been one hell of a year for me. First I lost my scouting job with the army, now this."

"You lost your job?"

"A snotty major at Fort Leavenworth gave me my walking papers after he found me passed out behind the stable from too much red-eye. Claimed it was one time too many, that the army didn't abide heavy drinkers." Reardon snorted. "Hell, if it wasn't for the army, half the whiskey makers in this country would go out of business."

Now Fargo understood why the scout had been so upset when the earl threatened to complain to friends in the government. Once Reardon's record came to light, there would be a formal investigation and Reardon might be sacrificed to pacify the earl.

"That rotten major was a tea guzzler, I'd bet," Reardon was saying. "It's always those do-good types who go around making life miserable for the rest of us."

Three miles from the camp they came on a few stragglers from the buffalo herd. Five cows and a calf were grazing on a hillock to the north, and as soon as Fargo laid eyes on them he pulled out the Sharps and bore down at a gallop. Several of the cows looked up, flicked their short tails, and were off. Reardon let loose a bloodcurdling bellow that spooked the rest.

Fargo selected the biggest cow as his target. The distance was still too great so he held his fire, hoping he could overtake her before they came in sight of the herd. The last thing he wanted was to cause another stampede.

For half a mile the chase went on, until at last Fargo reined up sharply, bringing the stallion to a sliding halt. He tucked the stock to his shoulder, pulled back the hammer, and sighted deliberately. At the crack of the Sharps the cow stumbled, pitched onto her front knees, and rolled head over hooves.

Fargo spurred the pinto on and fed a new cartridge into the Sharps. Behind him the scout's rifle cracked and another cow dropped. This time it was the calf's mother. The calf immediately stopped, hurried to her side, and tried to nuzzle her to life. The scout's next shot knocked it onto her flank.

The remaining buffalo fled westward until they were lost to view. Fargo swung down near the cow he had shot and warily advanced to verify she was dead. Loud wheezing told him she still had some life in her, and as he raised the Sharps the cow lifted its ponderous head, saw him, and heaved to her feet. Lowering her head, she charged.

Fargo planted a slug squarely between her eyes, felling

her before she could get up steam. Fingers flying, he re-loaded, but a third shot proved unnecessary. He turned and saw Reardon forty feet away, leaning down to examine the other two.

The scout smiled and held up an arm. "Not bad. This should make enough jerky to last those greenhorns halfway to Kansas City."

At that moment there was a single sharp retort from far off and Fargo saw Ben Reardon jerk, then take a short, stiff step. Astonishment replaced the scout's smile and Reardon slowly crumpled, staring down at a gaping hole in the middle of his chest. His horse bolted.

Spinning, Fargo crouched, the Sharps at the ready. On a hill to the northeast sunlight glinted off metal. He threw himself to one side as the earth next to his boot spewed into the air. Rolling behind the cow, he pushed up and rested the barrel of his rifle across her body.

Another shot sounded. The Ovaro nickered and side-stepped a dozen feet. Fargo jumped up to go after the pinto, but a bullet tore into the ground at his very toes, driving him to cover. Thwarted, afraid the stallion would be shot if it stayed there and unable to reach it without taking a bullet himself, he tore out a clump of grass and threw the clod, yelling, "Go on! Get!"

The Ovaro trotted off, its mane flying.

To Fargo's relief, the sniper let the horse go. He hunkered close to the cow and surveyed the hill, but all he could see was high grass. Either the killer was lying low, waiting for him to blunder and show himself, or else the man was working toward him for a clear shot.

Fargo stared at Reardon, prone in a spreading puddle of blood. Who was to blame? he wondered. One of the earl's bunch? And if so, which one, and why? None of them had been very fond of the scout, but not one had cause to kill him except Ashley Hadden, and Fargo couldn't imagine the earl committing cold-blooded murder over a few heated words. But he had to admit he could be wrong.

The sun blazed mercilessly on the prairie. Lying there in the blistering heat, Fargo soon had a dry throat and was caked with perspiration. He removed his hat to wipe his brow, then replaced it. To add to his discomfort, the powerful odor of the cow, combined with the scent of blood and urine, caused him to take shallow breaths. Flies gathered swiftly, ringing the bullet holes.

Fargo couldn't count on anyone coming from the camp. They wouldn't miss him until after dark, and by then it would be all over. Unless he cared to spend the whole day baking, he had to carry the fight to the bushwhacker.

Flattening, Fargo crawled into the grass, creeping eastward toward the cow and calf shot by Reardon. From a different angle he might be able to spot the killer. He held the Sharps close to his side so there would be no reflection of sunshine to give him away. Halfway there the stillness was broken by a high-pitched shriek, and peering skyward he beheld a lone red hawk winging in a circle above the hill. Whoever had taken the shots was still there.

The cow and calf were lying in a clear area. Fargo skirted around to a point opposite the hill, then rose onto his hands and knees and flew the final few yards. He reached the safety of the cow and hunkered down.

Removing his hat again, Fargo inched his head high enough to see the crown of the hill clearly. At first he saw nothing except grass and weeds, but after close study he made out the vague outline of a long dark shape near the top. Resting the Sharps on the cow's shoulder, he adjusted the rifle's sights to take into account the elevation and took precise aim on the center of the figure.

Fargo held his breath, relaxed his arms, and when the Sharps was perfectly steady, he fired. On the hill the figure leaped erect, a hand pressed to his side, and raced off. Fargo caught a glimpse of a suit and a hat such as the Englishmen wore, then the man had gone to ground again.

Dashing around the buffalo, Fargo sprinted toward the hill, reloading on the run. He had to jump over Reardon's body and saw the scout's wide-open eyes staring blankly up at him. Bending low, Fargo weaved while keeping his gaze fixed on the top of the hill. As a result, he nearly missed seeing the man when the bushwhacker popped up on the right slope. Taking one more stride, he threw himself forward.

The shot buzzed overhead. Fargo flipped to the left, squatted, and aimed, but as he prepared to fire his rifle the figure disappeared once more. Fargo ran on, veering toward the left slope. He had over eighty yards to cover and was certain the man would try to get off another shot, but he reached the base of the hill without seeing the Englishman.

Fargo crouched to catch his breath. He heard hoofbeats and shifted to find the Ovaro returning. Afraid the killer might shoot the pinto to strand him there, Fargo anxiously scanned the hill, coiled to fire at the first hint of movement. But the Englishman still failed to appear.

Once the stallion stopped in front of him, Fargo quickly vaulted into the saddle and took off up the hill at a gallop. He was tired of playing hide-and-seek. It was time to take the fight to the bushwhacker, and to that end he sped to the crest and looked to the right and the left, the rifle at his shoulder.

The Englishman had fled. A quarter of a mile to the east his thoroughbred was raising puffs of dust.

Fargo jabbed his spurs and went in pursuit. The Ovaro had seldom been matched against a horse of such high caliber, and Fargo had no idea whether he could catch the man or not. But he was going to give it his best try. Shoving the Sharps into his saddle scabbard, he knuckled down to the business of riding.

Soon it became apparent that the Englishman was aware of being chased. He lashed his horse furiously with his reins and removed his hat to slap its neck. The animal seemed to have wings on its feet, the way it glided through the high grass.

Undaunted, Fargo stretched the pinto to its limit, and beyond. The stallion had never let him down yet, not against fleet Indian ponies, full-blooded palominos, or half-wild mustangs. And now he was gratified to find the Ovaro was slowly but surely gaining on the thoroughbred.

Fargo was mystified when the Englishman unaccountably slanted to the northeast. The camp lay to the southeast, and by all rights that was where the man should be headed. Unless, of course, the killer didn't want anyone else to know what had happened.

For minutes on end the two horses sped across the plain, the Englishman handling his mount well but awkwardly. Fargo realized the man was favoring one arm, no doubt because of the wound inflicted by the Sharps. Steadily closer he drew, until—when the Englishman glanced back for the umpteenth time—Fargo recognized the rider as another of the earl's bodyguards, a young man named Roberts.

Fargo hardly knew him. They had exchanged a half-dozen words the whole time Fargo had been with the nobleman's party. Why then had the bodyguard tried to kill him? Why kill Ben Reardon? There were so many questions Fargo needed to have answered, and here was his chance if he could just take Roberts alive.

Fargo skirted an earthen mound and reached for his Colt, thinking he could wing the man. Suddenly more mounds appeared, scores and scores of them, dotting the prairie like oversized pimples. Knowing what they meant, he hauled on the reins, slowing the Ovaro.

The Englishman was already well into the middle of the prairie-dog town, the agile rodents venting their shrill whistles as they scattered pell-mell from his path. He ignored them and their burrows, and in doing so made a rash mistake that was costly for both him and his horse. Moments later the thoroughbred stepped into one of the holes, its leg wedged fast, and down it went, squealing in agony as the bone snapped clean in half below the knee.

Roberts went sailing over the animal's head and smacked to the earth on his chest. Rising unsteadily, he took a few faltering steps, then collapsed.

Fargo picked his way inward with caution. A few prairie dogs peeked out of their holes to watch him go by, chattering angrily at the intrusion. He dismounted near the thrashing thoroughbred, drew his Colt, and advanced to the bodyguard.

Roberts was on his left side, groaning. Blood seeped from his nose and the corners of his mouth. Fargo dropped to one knee and prodded Roberts with the six-shooter, but the man showed no reaction. Opening several shirt buttons, Fargo had to take only one look to see the man's chest had been caved in by the spill. The Englishman would be lucky if he lived out the hour.

Replacing the Colt, Fargo probed the man's clothes and found a pistol in a shoulder holster, another of the Tranter double-action .43-caliber models favored by the earl's men.

The revolver lacked the graceful lines of a Colt, and the butt was too narrow for his taste. He jammed it under his belt as he walked to the thoroughbred.

The horse looked up fearfully, its eyes wide, nostrils flaring. It made a valiant effort to jerk its leg free, but already the swelling had rendered the task impossible.

"Sorry, fella," Fargo said, shucking the Sharps. He never had liked having to put a horse out of its misery, but when it had to be done, he preferred to do the job with a single, painless shot. Touching the barrel to the thoroughbred's ear, he sent a slug through its brain.

At the blast the Englishman's eyes snapped open and he tried to sit up, but couldn't. Slumping flat, he stared at his horse, then at Fargo. He had to try several times before he croaked, "Thanks, Yank. That was bloody decent of you."

Fargo went over. "There's one thing I have to know. Why? What did I ever do to you?"

"Not me," Roberts said weakly, his eyelids quivering. "The countess."

Fargo wondered if the man had seen him kiss Kendra Hadden, but he dismissed the notion on recalling that Roberts had been off with Oakley, watering the horses. "Explain yourself," he said.

"You know what I meant," Roberts declared. He tried to speak again. The exertion drained his face of color and caused him to cough up more blood instead.

"I need to know," Fargo persisted when the fit was over. "First Moulton, now you. Who is behind this? Who wants me dead?"

"They all would if they knew."

"Knew what, damn it?"

Roberts closed his eyes and exhaled. "We English won't stand for such a thing. It's for her own good, really."

"What is?" Fargo demanded, grasping the bodyguard's arm.

"You'd be better off leaving," Roberts said, the words barely audible. "There will be others out to get you if you don't."

Since he was getting nowhere, Fargo tried to learn the truth another way. "What about Reardon? Why did you kill him? What did he have to do with the countess?"

"Nothing," Roberts answered softly. "Couldn't leave a witness." He commenced coughing again and his body went into severe convulsions that lasted a good long while. When they ended, he gave out a gurgling gasp, went rigid, and died.

Fargo slowly rose. Once again fate had cheated him. All he had learned was that there would be other attempts on his life so long as he stayed with the earl's outfit. He had to uncover the reason soon, before one of those tries was successful.

8

It was after midnight and Skye Fargo lay on his back on his blankets, pondering the day's events, when he detected the light tread of someone sneaking toward him. Silently he drew the Colt and moved close to his saddle for cover. Thumb on the hammer, he rose until he spotted a shapely figure topped by a mane of long hair. For a moment he thought it was Kendra, but a whisper showed otherwise.

"Hi there, handsome. I couldn't sleep."

Flora Livingstone, wearing a loose-fitting robe and slippers, sat down on the blankets and rested her hands on her knees. "Is that how you greet your ladyfriends?" she asked, nodding at the six-gun.

Fargo twirled the Colt into his holster. "I can't be any too careful."

"No, I suppose not," Flora said. "I still can't get over what happened. That Mr. Reardon wasn't such a bad bloke once you got to know him."

"Maybe you should go on back," Fargo suggested. "I don't want you to take a bullet meant for me." He surveyed the camp, which was still and peaceful under the pale light from the quarter-moon. Thirty feet away stood the wagon, around which slept the surviving Britishers, all except for a single sentry who sat near the three racks of smoked buffalo meat.

"Don't worry on that score. Everyone besides Oakley is in dreamland," Flora said. "I checked." Her mouth curved in a seductive grin. "I didn't want to be disturbed."

"I'm glad you came," Fargo said. "I can't sleep anyway." He took her hand, paused to stare at the sleeping form of Kendra Hadden, then led her into the grass a safe distance.

Flora's arms crept around his neck and she kissed him

lightly on the lips. "You can't imagine how much I've wanted another go at you. The last time just whetted my appetite." She began to lower her mouth to his neck, but he held a finger to her lips.

"First things first. Have you heard anything that would interest me?"

"Not a clue, luv," Flora said. "As hard as it is to believe, I don't think the earl was involved with the attempt on your life. I listened to the talk at supper, and you should have seen how Kendra grilled him. Unless he's a lot better liar than I give him credit for being, he's as much in the dark as you are."

"Keep your ears open. Maybe you'll learn something."

"For you, anything," Flora said. She gave his buttock a playful tweak. "Now enough of this chitchat. There's more important business to attend to." With that, she opened the front of her robe to reveal she was naked underneath. "See what I mean, big man?"

Fargo grinned and reached up to cup her breasts. They were full and round, the peaks hardening under his light touch. He bent to suck on her left nipple, rolling the tip with his tongue. Above him Flora panted softly and ran her fingers through his hair.

"Lord, you make me tingle all over."

Fargo changed to her right nipple and pinched it between his lips while roaming his hands lower, over her flat belly to the hairy junction of her thighs. A bit lower and he could feel the heat radiating from her womanhood. Her thighs trembled as he massaged them, and when he eased a finger nearer her core, she moaned and gripped his hair so hard it hurt.

"Nice and slow, lover," Flora said. "I want to remember this for a long time."

Obligingly, Fargo moved at a snail's pace, worming his right hand to the heavy, wet lips of her sex. Here he stroked her with the slightest pressure, causing her to gush, "Ohhh-hhhhhh!"

Fargo dallied, drawing out her pleasure. She squirmed against him, her breasts jiggling, then opened her legs, hiked her bottom, and literally sucked his forefinger inside of her. He wiggled it, making her shudder with passion, and moved his other hand around to clasp her backside. "Like that?" he asked.

"You have no idea!"

Stooping, Fargo bent her backward until he bore her full weight on his forearm. The cool grass yielded as he gently laid her down. Positioning himself between her bent legs, he trailed his tongue from her twin mounds to her navel. Her skin rippled under him, and when he licked in a circle on her stomach, her hips gave a little jump.

Fargo slipped a second finger into her slick tunnel. Flora voiced a tiny cry and lifted her hips into the air, grinding into him. He clamped his fingers together and slid them all the way in and then almost all the way out, doing this over and over again, the friction stoking her inner flames. Her inner walls clung to his fingers, and soft mewing came from deep in her throat.

After a bit, Fargo substituted his mouth for his fingers. The instant his tongue bored into her, Flora arched her spine and came off the ground as if trying to take flight.

"Ah! Ah! Ah! Don't stop! Ever!"

Fargo licked and flicked to his heart's content, and all the while Flora's nails bit into his back, his shoulders, his neck. She strained her bottom to move with him, lashing it back and forth and up and down in a frenzy of carnal lust. Her dank scent filled his nostrils and made his mouth water.

"Ummmmmmm!" Flora crooned.

Only when Fargo's tongue grew sore did he rise up, unbuckle his belt and his gun belt, and position himself on his knees. Flora reached down, took the tip of his manhood, and rubbed it against her nether lips, which excited her more. Her fingers traced delicate paths the length of his pole, sending exquisite shivers coursing through his body.

Fargo kissed her breasts again, then found her moist lips. Her mouth molded to his as if the two were one, and her tongue tangled with his own in an erotic dance. He parted her thighs wide, aligned his manhood, and rammed it into her to the hilt. Flora tossed back her head and crammed a hand into her mouth to stifle a scream that would have brought every last member of the earl's entourage on the run.

Placing his palms flat, Fargo levered his body in a rocking motion, his toes giving him an added measure of thrust. Flora rolled her head back and forth in a delirium of pleasure, her hand still sandwiched between her gleaming teeth. Her legs swept up and around, her ankles locked on his back.

Fargo was in no rush. He pumped in a smooth motion, his pole pulsing, his mouth lathering her face, her throat, her earlobes. She responded by gripping his head and hungrily gluing her lips to his. Her behind bucked in time to the tempo of his strokes.

Their mutual climax was a long time coming. Fargo held off until Flora showed the familiar signs he had been waiting for; her head snapped back, her body shook uncontrollably, and her insides spurted. He let himself go, relishing the potent release, listening to the slap-slap-slap of their stomachs.

"Yes! Yes! Yes!"

Fargo couldn't agree more. He drained himself dry and slowly coasted to a stop, settling on top of her ripe melons. Flora unhooked her legs and relaxed, her fingers at the nape of his neck. She kissed his head, his ear.

"The countess doesn't know what she's missing."

"Oh?"

"I know she wants you. I've seen how she looks at you when she thinks you're not watching. But she's too much the lady to break her marriage vows." Flora paused. "The earl is a bloody fool to neglect her like he does. She's given him every chance to mend his ways, but he can't be bothered."

"Does he have another woman somewhere?"

"I've wondered about that," Flora said. "But I honestly don't think he does. He's a strange duck, that one. If he shares his bed with her once a year, he believes that's enough."

Fargo felt himself dozing off and didn't resist. He could feel Flora winding his hair around her fingers and the gentle caress of the breeze on his back. In the distance an owl hooted and was answered by another farther away. Instantly he sat bolt upright, scouring the prairie.

"What the devil!" Flora exclaimed.

"Hush," Fargo said sternly.

"What's the matter?" she whispered.

"Indians." Fargo dressed swiftly, palmed his six-shooter, and grasped her arm. "Stay low and don't talk." He headed back, halting every few yards to listen. The hoots were not repeated and they reached the camp safely.

"Should I wake the others?" Flora inquired.

"No. But send Oakley over." Fargo gave her a pat on the rump as she turned, then he moved his saddle and bedding closer to the horses. As he was smoothing the blankets, the bodyguard approached.

"You wanted to see me, sir?"

"We have company," Fargo said, and explained.

"I say!" Oakley stated, swiveling on a heel, his Tranter out in a flash. "The blighters must be watching us this very second! We have to rouse the rest, build up the fire, post guards—"

"Don't go off half-cocked," Fargo interrupted. "Most Indians don't like to attack at night, so there's no need to start a panic."

"But—"

Fargo held up a hand. "If I'm right, there are just two of them, Arapahos sent to keep an eye on us. Now that our numbers have been whittled down, I wouldn't be surprised if the band I saw doesn't aim to steal our horses and take a few scalps. In the next day or two they'll strike."

"What do we do, then?"

"You go back to the fire and act like nothing is wrong," Fargo said. "I'm about to lie down and let them think I've fallen asleep."

Oakley reluctantly slid the Tranter under his jacket. "You're going out there after them, aren't you?"

"Anything I can do now to cut down the odds will help us in the long run," Fargo answered. "And it will give us a head start."

"I'd be honored to go with you."

"No. You have to be ready to warn the others in case I don't come back." Fargo sat and wrapped a blanket over his legs. "Keep the fire low so they can't see too clearly."

"I will. And good luck."

Reclining on his saddle, Fargo pulled his hat brim low

over his eyes and yawned loudly. He had the Sharps at his side and his right hand was close to the Colt. Peeking under his hat, he scoured the grass, but as he expected, he did not see the watching warriors. They were too shrewd for that.

Time dragged by. Fargo made a point of tossing every so often, and on his last turn he contrived to slip low to the ground so that no one could see his next move. He glanced at the horses, all of which were dozing, then leaving his hat propped on the saddle, he slid into the buffalo grass.

Fargo brought his right leg close to his waist and grabbed the Arkansas toothpick. The work he had to do must be done silently. If the first warrior managed to cry out, the second would race to Eagle Claw and before the next day was done the Britishers would be attacked.

He crawled a few feet at a time, his ears tuned to the night sounds, to the chirp of crickets and the distant yip of coyotes. Based on the owl hoots he had heard, he guessed that one of the Arapahos was north of the camp, the other to the south. He could only hope they were the only two.

The silent stalk was nerve-wracking, and made more so by the fact that the Arapahos were every bit Fargo's equal. Their senses might be even sharper. He couldn't relax his vigilance for a second, and he dared not make a single sound that could be heard more than a few feet away.

Fargo slowly circled the camp. He had gone thirty yards and was of a mind to move farther out into the grass when an owl hooted not ten feet from where he was concealed. Across the clearing a second owl replied.

The warrior was much nearer to the edge of the grass than Fargo had figured on. He crept forward like a human tortoise, planting each limb with extreme care, bending the stems under him so that none rustled or crackled. All the while he kept his eyes fixed straight ahead, seeking the brave.

The wind picked that moment to intensify. In a sudden gust, the grass in front of Fargo parted and there was the Arapaho, crouched eight feet away. Fargo took advantage of the noise and immediately sprang. The toothpick in his right hand, he streaked the blade at the brave's ribs from behind.

Somehow, the warrior knew. He started to whirl, his right hand rising with a tomahawk in its grasp.

Fargo drove the toothpick in under the brave's arm and felt the blade slice through muscular flesh. It glanced off a rib and came close to being jarred loose. Fargo pivoted, his left hand covering the warrior's mouth before the man could yell. An elbow slammed into him and the brave tried to open his skull with the tomahawk.

Together they toppled. Fargo was on top. Ripping the toothpick out, he stabbed again. The Arapaho lifted the tomahawk for another blow, but death claimed him before he could complete the swing and he went as limp as a wet rag.

Fargo slid off, then wiped his knife on the man's leggings. He would have to bury the body later so Eagle Claw couldn't find it. Picking up the tomahawk, he was set to move off when from the south came another owl hoot.

It was the other warrior. The brave would know something was wrong if there was no answer, so doing the best he could, Fargo imitated the hoot he had heard just a short while ago. No response was forthcoming and he assumed his ruse had worked.

Fargo bore westward in a wide loop that eventually brought him up on the camp from the south. He planned to dispose of the second Arapaho as he had the first, but the unforeseen cropped up in the form of a ground-hitched paint pony. The horse spotted him at the same time he spotted it. He fell flat but he was too slow.

The paint voiced a low whinny, and at the limits of Fargo's vision a ghostly shape detached itself from a clump of weeds and vanished, blending into the night as if swallowed by the very air.

Fargo moved to the right, a shadow among the shadows. He kept one eye on the paint in case the warrior tried to escape, and he was due east of the pony when he realized the horse had been looking right at him the entire time. The Arapaho would know exactly where he was.

As that thought crossed Fargo's mind, a heavy body slammed into his back and a knife lanced past his face. The only reason the blade missed was because the impact snapped his head to one side. He landed on his hands and knees, stunned. An iron arm curled around his neck, choking off his breath, and he was yanked upward.

It was the same situation as with the first warrior, only in reverse. Fargo barely got an arm up to block the next thrust of the warrior's knife. As it was the blade nicked his forearm, drawing blood. He managed to take a short step and bent at the waist, throwing all of his weight into a shoulder throw. The brave flew up and over.

Fargo straightened as the Arapaho hit and rebounded with the agility of a wildcat. The warrior's knife flicked out and Fargo parried with the toothpick. Simultaneously, Fargo swung the tomahawk he still held at the brave's leg. The Arapaho twisted, skipped aside, and closed in again.

Fargo back-pedaled before a flurry of swings and stabs that would have sliced open a lesser fighter. Repeatedly he tried to bury either of his weapons in his foe; repeatedly the Arapaho blocked him or ducked or dodged.

Fargo tried a feint but the crafty warrior didn't fall for the trick. He aimed overhand and underhand strikes, none of which scored. There could be no doubt Fargo had met his match. Perhaps more than his match, judging by the skill the brave displayed.

The end came abruptly, unexpectedly. Fargo was still retreating before the Arapaho's fierce onslaught when from the edge of the grass Oakley called out, "Jump aside, Yank, and I'll shoot him for you!"

Startled, the warrior paused, glancing toward the Englishman, and in that frozen instant of time Fargo gave the toothpick a quick flip and grasped the blade instead of the hilt. Then, with a rapid downward motion, he hurled the throwing knife into the brave's chest.

The Arapaho grunted, staggered backward, and gripped the hilt. With a mighty wrench he tore the knife out, casting it to the ground. Whirling, he sprinted toward the paint.

Fargo had to stop him. He ran, hefting the tomahawk loosely in his right hand. Just as the Arapaho reached the paint and began to swing up, Fargo stopped, braced himself, and threw the tomahawk as he had hurled countless others while living with the Sioux. His cast was flawless. The keen edge bit into the Arapaho between the shoulder blades and the man stiffened, lost his grip on the paint, and fell. In four bounds Fargo reached him.

The warrior was on his side, trying in vain to seize the

tomahawk and tear it loose. He realized Fargo was there, glared in defiance, then glanced around for his knife, which he had dropped. He spied it and was extending his arm when a rifle shot rang out. The slug caught him below the left eye, snapping his head back, and he sank to the soil without a sound.

"I got the savage!" Oakley declared, hastening forward. He had removed his arm from the sling to shoot and he was rubbing his shoulder where the recoil had jarred it. "I heard a ruckus out here and came to investigate. Are you all right, Yank?"

"A few scratches is all," Fargo answered, stooping to retrieve the toothpick. Shouts had erupted in the camp and some of the Britishers were hurrying over.

"What about the other one?"

Fargo slashed a finger across his throat.

"Bloody hell! I didn't hear a thing."

"That was the idea."

Ashley Hadden, rifle in hand, was the first to arrive, with Revis, Hollis, Jeems, and two of the wounded men hard on his heels. They ringed the Arapaho, studying him. Last to show were the three women, each bundled in a blanket.

Fargo's eyes met those of the countess and lingered. She swallowed, pulling the blanket tighter around her as if to screen her body from his frank appraisal, but it had the opposite effect, accenting both the enticing swell of her bosom and the suggestive curve of her thighs.

"I demand an explanation," the earl hissed. "Where did this red devil come from?"

Fargo told Hadden about hearing the owls and stalking the two warriors.

"I can't believe you didn't inform me first," Hadden said sourly. "You put all of our lives at risk. What if you had been killed? Or what if you had been wrong and there had been more than two? Every last one of us could have been butchered in our sleep because of your incompetence."

"Fargo did what he thought was best, dear," Kendra said.

Hadden pivoted, and for a second he appeared on the verge of punching her. "I shouldn't be surprised you would leap to his defense. But I'll remind you that I'm in charge here, and that I should be posted on all new developments. Or is that too much to ask?"

"No, of course not," Kendra said.

The earl frowned and faced Fargo. "In the future, kindly refrain from these heroics unless you are under specific orders to do so."

"You keep forgetting," Fargo said as he slid the toothpick into his ankle sheath. "I'm not at your beck-and-call like the others. I can do as I damn well please."

Hadden had the aspect of a mad dog about to pounce. He restrained himself with a visible effort and slowly lowered his rifle. "How true. I shouldn't have snapped at you. Blame the strain we're all under."

Fargo took hold of the paint's rope reins and handed them to Oakley. "Take this one back while I go find the other one."

"Why bother?" the earl cut in. "We don't need them. We have more than enough horses as it is."

"If a riderless horse strays back to the Arapaho camp, they'll know something is wrong and come looking for us," Fargo responded.

Oakley regarded the dead brave. "Won't they come looking anyway when these two don't show?"

Fargo shrugged. "That depends on whether these two were to report back or just keep an eye on us until the band catches up." He walked off, saying over a shoulder, "I might have bought us a day or two, at the most. Sooner or later we'll tangle with them."

"I refuse to wait around helplessly, like sheep for the slaughter," Hadden said. "There must be something we can do."

"Keep your guns handy," Fargo advised.

Finding the first Arapaho was easy. Finding his mount was not. Fargo hunted and hunted in an ever-widening pattern but turned up no trace of the animal. The Britishers were gathered around the fire, sipping coffee, when he brought the bad tidings.

"Does this mean we can expect them that much sooner?" Flora wanted to know.

"Maybe," Fargo said. He turned to Ashley Hadden. "It

might be wise for us to forget about your bull for the time being and stick close to the wagon."

"Are you daft?" the earl retorted. "My collection won't be complete without it. No, nothing short of the end of the world will stop me from bagging my buffalo."

"Perhaps your death will," Fargo said, but the earl only laughed.

9

A gleaming vault of golden sun crowned the eastern horizon when the battered wagon rattled into motion, heading out toward Kansas City. Skye Fargo sat on the Ovaro, his brawny hands on the saddle horn, watching as the small column of riders and horses followed. Flora waved at him and he returned the gesture. Kendra Hadden looked back and merely nodded, yet there was a world of hidden meaning in the appeal in her eyes.

Ashley Hadden did not appear to notice. He gave his thoroughbred a smack and wheeled the animal to the west, remarking, "At last they're on their way. Let's enjoy ourselves, shall we?"

"Aren't you the least bit worried the Arapahos will harm your wife?" Fargo inquired, pacing the nobleman.

"We'll catch up with them by nightfall if all goes well," Hadden said. "Oakley and the others will watch over her until then."

"You didn't answer my question," Fargo said, tugging on the rope that was leading the three extra horses they had brought along.

"My feelings for my wife are none of your business," the earl said. "And I don't care to spoil my day by starting it with an argument. So let's drop the subject and concentrate on locating my bull."

First they had to locate the herd, which had drifted to the southwest during the past twenty-four hours. Fargo had no trouble following the spoor, and by the middle of the morning a large group of shaggy brutes was silhouetted on the horizon. The earl produced a field glass and inspected the animals closely, then remarked, "Damn. My bull isn't among them. We'll have to keep looking."

More buffalo were found, but each time it was the same. The earl would shake his head and ride on. Fargo's patience lasted until shortly before noon, at which point he reined up and announced, "This is a waste of time."

The nobleman halted. "I beg your pardon?"

"There must be fifty thousand animals in this herd. We could look from now until doomsday and not find the one you're after."

"I refuse to give up so easily."

Fargo motioned at several hundred beasts grazing a few hundred yards distant. "Just pick the biggest one you see and we'll be done with it."

Ashley Hadden shook his head. "You don't seem to understand. I can't shoot any old bull. It has to be the largest there is to do justice to my trophy wall. No sportsman would settle for less than the very best." He patted his rifle. "In Africa I shot an elephant with tusks twice the average size. The rhino I bagged had a horn as thick as your arm and half as long. In India I brought down a tiger so big his paws were as wide as your head. So you see, I need to find that bull."

Another hour went by, and another. Fargo kept thinking of Kendra and Flora, of their certain fate if Eagle Claw caught up with them before he did. He chafed at the delay, and he was about ready to tell the nobleman to go to hell and just leave when Hadden cackled with delight as he pointed at another cluster of animals a quarter of a mile to the west.

"There! There he is! As magnificent as I remembered!"

Fargo was offered the field glass. Sure enough, an enormous bull stood head and shoulders above the rest of the herd. Unfortunately, it was surrounded by dozens of cows, calves, and smaller bulls. Getting near enough for a clear shot would be next to impossible, and he commented to that effect.

"There has to be a way," Hadden said. "We could chase it until it's exhausted and finish it at our leisure."

"And maybe start another stampede. Do you want to go through that again?"

"Come up with a better idea, then. You're the professional."

Fargo rode southward, staying far enough from the buffalo so as not to spook them but close enough to find the other animals he was after, predators that constantly prowled the fringes of the great herds seeking unguarded calves, the aged, and the sick. He had spotted a small pack earlier, and now, from the top of a knoll, he lifted a hand and said, "There."

"What?" Hadden asked. "All I see are wolves."

"Shoot one."

"Why on earth should I do that?"

"You want to get close to the bull, don't you?" Fargo said irritably. "Indians use this trick all the time. First they shoot a wolf, then they skin it and cover themselves with the hide."

"Oh! I get it. A disguise," Hadden said. "I'll be able to crawl right up to that old monster." His head suddenly snapped up and he gazed past Fargo, shielding his eyes with a hand. "I say. Are they who I think they are?"

Fargo swiveled, counted six Arapahos approaching at a gallop, and barked, "Ride for your life!" Suiting action to words, he raced southward, hauling on the lead rope. A chorus of war whoops greeted their flight.

"Where did they come from?" The earl had to shout to be heard above the pounding of hooves.

The same question troubled Fargo. Either the six had struck their trail by accident, or the warriors had been shadowing them since sunrise. And there was another matter to consider. Eagle Claw's band had consisted of sixteen warriors, two of whom were now dead. Which meant eight were unaccounted for and might be attacking the rest of the Britishers at that very moment.

Fargo had to continually tug on the rope so the extra horses would keep up. He saw the six Arapahos gaining, knew he could not possibly outrun them encumbered with the extras, and dropping the rope, allowed the stallion to fly like the wind.

"What are you doing?" Hadden roared. "Do you have any idea how much those thoroughbreds cost?"

"Catch them if you want," Fargo shot back.

An arrow whizzed through the air between them and impaled itself in the sod, nipping in the bud whatever response the earl was about to make. Hunching low, he worked his reins with vigor.

Fargo surveyed the terrain in front of them, looking for a place to make a stand, somewhere to hold the Indians at bay. He had let go of the spare horses too late. But there were no trees anywhere, no hills or gullies. All he spied were buffalo wallows.

They would have to do. Fargo angled to the nearest one, a saucer-shaped depression ten feet wide and over a foot deep. He reined up in the middle, shucked the Sharps, and leaped down. Grabbing the reins, he smacked the pinto's front legs and the Ovaro obediently sank to its knees.

Ashley Hadden had followed, but he was gazing around in confusion. "We shouldn't stop," he said, and was lifting his reins when another shaft flashed out of the blue and thudded into the side of his mount. Neighing wildly, the horse tottered. Hadden attempted to right it and had almost succeeded when an arrow transfixed the animal's neck. Snorting and kicking, the horse collapsed.

By then Fargo was at the rim of the bowl and curling back the hammer on his Sharps. He sighted on the lead warrior, the bowman, as the brave notched a fourth shaft. The Arapaho elevated the bow and aimed, but the blast of Fargo's shot rolled across the plain first and the warrior dropped.

The five remaining braves scattered right and left. In moments they had blended into the grass.

Fargo hunkered down and reloaded. He saw the nobleman vainly trying to get the stricken thoroughbred back on its feet. "Your horse is a goner," he said. "Get down or you'll be the same."

As if to accent the point, an arrow whizzed into the wallow, narrowly missing the Ovaro. Ashley Hadden, wide-eyed, squatted and scooted over.

Fargo had thrown the rifle to his shoulder. He had a fair idea of where the archer was hiding and he sent a slug in that direction to discourage another attempt.

The earl scoured the prairie. "Where are they? I don't see a thing."

"You won't, until it's too late."

"Why did you trap us in this stinking hole?" Hadden asked. "We should have kept on riding."

"We lost too much ground trying to save those horses of yours," Fargo answered. "Once the Arapahos were in bow range, we had to take cover."

"And now we're pinned down with no hope of escape," Hadden grumbled.

"We will try once its dark."

"Provided we live that long, you cretin."

Skye Fargo had tolerated more badgering from the Earl of Somerset than he had from any other man in a long time. Partly because he knew the nobleman was from a different country and didn't know any better, and partly due to his feelings for Kendra, he had let the heckling go unpunished. But suddenly, as he knelt there staring at the earl's hate-filled features, something snapped inside of him and he hauled off and punched the Englishman flush on the chin.

Caught off guard, Hadden sprawled on his back and lay there, stunned.

Fargo turned back to the plain, making a three-hundred-and-sixty-degree scan. The Arapahos were well concealed, but their horses were still out in the open. He considered shooting the mounts so the warriors would be left on foot when he made his break on the Ovaro. Doing so, though, would only enrage them and might spark another attack. He chose to hold off.

The earl groaned, then slowly sat up, rubbing his chin and glowering. "You dirty bastard," he hissed. "I should have expected an underhanded blow like that. You're not gentleman enough to fight fairly."

"Anytime, anyplace," Fargo said.

A wily grin lit Hadden's face. "I'll hold you to your bravado. Once we're safe, I plan to give you the thrashing of your life."

"Like you do to your wife every time you're in a bad mood?"

Hadden flushed scarlet, grabbed his rifle, and made as if to spring. At the last instant he caught himself and settled for sneering. "As you're so fond of saying, I can do as I damn well please. She's my wife, and if she displeases me enough to merit a beating, that's my affair."

. "You're a jackass, mister. Most men would give their eyeteeth to be married to a fine woman like her."

"Shows how much you know. Kendra is a complete and utter bore. She can't stand to hunt. She dislikes travel. At social functions she's a shy wallflower. I did her a favor by taking her as my wife."

Fargo was busy scouring the grass. As much as he would have liked to give the nobleman a piece of his mind, he pointed at the far side of the wallow and said, "Keep watch over there."

"I'm not done yet," Hadden said. "Don't think I haven't seen how you look at her. Don't think I don't know what is on your mind."

"*Not now*," Fargo uttered. He would have added more, but at that juncture an Arapaho appeared sixty yards out and jumped onto a war-horse. Sliding onto the off-side, the warrior goaded the animal into a trot, bearing eastward.

"Is the blighter running away?" the earl asked.

"He's going for help," Fargo said as he leveled the Sharps. Tracking the mount with his sights, he fired at a range of eighty-five yards. The warhorse crumpled, the rider disappearing before it touched the earth.

Seconds later, glittering arrows flew in from both sides, one clipping the dead thoroughbred, the other missing the Ovaro by inches. Fargo sent a shot at the bowman to the west. Hadden fired to the east. No more shafts were loosed, but Fargo doubted that either of them had hit either brave.

Leaning against the wallow rim, Fargo squinted up at the scorching sun, then at the hard mud lining the bottom of the depression. In no time they would be roasting. Reloading, he glanced at the earl and commented, "I thought I told you to do something."

Hadden showed his resentment, but he obeyed. Once he was squatting at the edge, he looked around and said warningly, "I want you to know that before I'm done with you, you'll be on your hands and knees begging me to spare your miserable life."

Fargo did not waste his breath responding, and that only angered the nobleman more.

"I should have had you stripped to the waist and whipped when I had the chance. My wife wouldn't think so highly of you once she saw you publicly humiliated." Hadden smirked. "I honestly can't understand what she sees in you. But I saw how she acted the day you showed up. I knew. Yet when I questioned her, she had the audacity to lie. I couldn't even beat the truth out of her."

"Why tell me all this?"

"Because I don't want you to think you pulled the wool over my eyes, you pathetic lout. I was on to you from the beginning."

"You put on quite an act."

"There was a reason I acted so friendly," Hadden said. "And you'll never know what it was." Falling silent, he turned and placed his rifle in front of him.

A soft rustling to the north caught Fargo's ear, but when he focused on the spot where it came from it had stopped. He suspected they had a long wait ahead of them, and he made himself comfortable after loosening the Colt in its holster. The stench from the bottom of the wallow was becoming more unbearable by the minute so he pulled his bandanna up over his mouth and nose.

The afternoon waned slowly. Not once did the Arapahos make their presence known. Out on the prairie their mounts gathered and grazed. To the north buffalo moved about. Occasionally a hawk or sparrow flew by.

Skye Fargo expected the attack to come shortly before sunset. The Arapahos were not about to let them leave the wallow alive, and under the cover of nightfall they could do just that. So he marked the passage of the sun with interest, and when there was less than an hour to go, he told Hadden, "They'll be on us soon."

"Good. I'm tired of all this waiting."

Slipping below the rim, Fargo changed position, moving a few yards to the right. He placed four cartridges in a neat row on the earthen lip and held a fifth in his left hand. He was being optimistic. When pressed, he could fire and reload in under ten seconds, so he might be able to get off two shots before the braves reached the wallow.

A coyote yipped to the east. Another answered from the west.

"Get ready," Fargo whispered.

The warning was timely. From out of the grass on two

sides flew the spinning shafts. One embedded itself near where Fargo had been lying. The second was meant for Ashley Hadden and it flew true, the barbed point digging a furrow in his upper arm. He grabbed the wound and fell, and as he did five shrieking warriors burst from cover and charged.

Fargo was ready. He centered the Sharps on the sternum of a bowman and stroked the trigger as the man let fly. Without bothering to verify the result, fingers a blur, he transferred the cartridge in his left hand to his right and levered the trigger guard. Skillfully he inserted the new bullet and rose to shoot again.

A warrior holding a lance was almost upon him. The Arapaho hoisted his weapon high, his shoulder muscles rippling, and poised for the throw.

Fargo was unable to take precise aim. He had to fire from the waist, the Sharps slanted upward, the stock tucked to his hip. The blast bowled the brave over, the .52-caliber slug tearing clear through him from navel to spine and leaving an exit hole the size of a fist.

A third warrior was rushing from the right, a war club upraised.

Rotating, Fargo brought the rifle up and deflected a vicious blow that would have caved in his forehead. The force behind it knocked him backward. He tried to keep the Sharps between them, but another blow battered it from his hands. Automatically he went for the Colt. His fingers were closing on the butt when the brave leaped, bearing him to the ground.

Fargo lunged and grabbed the Arapaho's wrist as the club arced at his temple. The warrior's other hand closed on his throat, fingernails digging deep. Fargo tried to tear the hand loose but the brave had sinews of iron.

Shoving hard, Fargo was able to separate them enough to raise his right leg and drive his knee into the Indian's side. The Arapahos grunted but clung on tenaciously. Struggling and tussling, they rolled back and forth, neither able to gain a decisive advantage.

Fargo was finding it harder and harder to breathe. He heaved, bucking like a bronc, yet all that accomplished was to enable the Arapaho to slide on top of him. Pinned, his lungs on fire with pain, he rammed his knee into the warrior's backbone twice in a row. At last the grip on his throat weakened.

But not enough. Fargo had to break that hold before he was throttled to death. He twisted his right foot so that his boot heel was toward the Arapaho, then drove his spur into the warrior's flesh.

The brave stiffened, let go, and flung himself to one side.

Both men scrambled to their feet and warily circled. Fargo could hear a fight going on behind him. Evidently the earl was holding his own against the last pair.

Hissing, the warrior with the club lunged and swung. Fargo danced aside, shifted, slapped leather, and put two slugs into the astonished Arapaho in the blink of an eye.

The brave tottered, his arms slumping, gaping at the smoking six-shooter. Refusing to give up, he gritted his teeth and lifted the club a final time.

Fargo fanned the Colt once. The slug spun the warrior completely around and dropped him where he stood. Whirling, Fargo was set to finish off the remaining braves. He need not have bothered.

The fourth Arapaho was already dead, lying on his back with his head bent at an outlandish angle.

The fifth Arapaho was locked in combat with Ashley Hadden who, although unarmed, was holding his own with surprising ease. The warrior had a knife and was stabbing and slashing in a fury. Hadden evaded every try, a mocking grin on his face.

Growing reckless, the Arapaho thrust too far forward, spearing his blade low, toward the Englishman's groin. Hadden slipped in, grasped the warrior's forearm, and pumped it as he might a pump handle. The brave did a somersault in the air and crashed down on his shoulders.

Fargo saw the earl take a hopping step, leap into the air, and spin. Hadden's foot rammed into the Arapaho as the man was rising, and the Arapaho went flying one way, his knife another. Swiftly Hadden moved in. The warrior, weaving groggily, tried to land several punches that Hadden countered with slapping motions. Then Hadden, his hands held rigid like spear tips, hit the brave twice in the ribs. The Arapaho fell to his knees and looked up in disbelief.

Ashley Hadden drew back his right hand, smiled, and swinging his arm as he might a sword, chopped the warrior across the throat.

The Arapaho gurgled and sputtered, his neck folding in upon itself. He pitched to the ground, twitched, and was dead.

A heady glow lit the Earl of Somerset's features as he turned. On seeing Fargo, he took a step, but stopped when his gaze fell to the Colt. He surveyed the wallow and nodded. "Looks like we taught these savages a lesson, eh?"

Fargo had never seen anyone fight like the earl before. He recalled Oakley telling him that the nobleman was a very dangerous man, a claim he had doubted until just now. "We were lucky," he answered.

"Rubbish. I make my own luck."

Reaching to his belt, Fargo palmed several cartridges and commenced reloading the six-gun. During the fight the Ovaro had risen and moved to the edge of the wallow. Now the stallion walked to him and nuzzled him as if to assure himself Fargo was unharmed.

The earl gave one of the Arapahos a kick, then snickered, "So much for the vaunted prowess of redskins. After all the stories I've heard about their savagery, I must confess to being disappointed."

Fargo's dislike of the man soared to new heights. Killing an enemy was one thing, gloating over it another. He finished with the Colt and took hold of the Ovaro's reins.

"At least we can get on with the business at hand," Hadden commented eagerly. "Catch me one of those Indians mounts and we'll go after my bull."

"No."

"My ears must not be working properly."

"You heard me," Fargo said as he stepped to the Sharps and picked it up.

Hadden advanced, lightning crackling from his eyes. "Why the hell not?"

"Eagle Claw had sixteen braves with him. Eight are still unaccounted for."

"So?"

"So where do you think they might be right this minute?" Fargo brushed dirt off the Sharps and shoved it into the scabbard. "I'll catch one of those ponies for you, but we're going to check on the women and the others, not waste time hunting your buffalo."

The earl stopped and placed his hands on his hips. "No one can say I haven't been patient with you," he said. "But a man has only so much patience and mine is at an end." He squared his shoulders. "You are long overdue to be taught to respect your betters." And with that, he jumped like a jackrabbit and kicked Fargo in the temple.

10

Skye Fargo had been about to climb on the stallion. His back was to the nobleman, and he was not expecting trouble so soon after the fight with the Arapahos. He did not see the kick coming, but he felt the jolting impact as he was thrown against the pinto. His vision swam and his knees began to buckle. Through sheer force of will he stayed upright, holding on to the saddle horn, then spun.

Ashley Hadden had retreated a yard and held his hands rigid once again, his arms bent at the elbows. "What's the matter, lout?" he taunted. "Can't you take a little pain?"

Anger make Fargo take a step and punch. He should have known better, for the next moment he was flying head over heels, coming to rest in the dust near the dead thoroughbred. Bruised and aching, he sat up and heard mocking laughter.

"Oh, please! Is this the best you can do? You're more pathetic than these worthless Indians."

Fargo's hat had fallen off but he did not reclaim it. Instead, standing slowly, he clenched both fists and moved toward the earl.

"I promised you this would happen," Hadden said gleefully. "You don't stand a prayer, and you're too stupid to realize it." He skipped to the left, sinking into an odd crouch, his hands close to his waist. "I was taught by Kano himself."

The name meant nothing to Fargo, but he had seen enough of the earl's ability to not take the man lightly. Crouching, so as not to leave his midsection open to one of those slashing hand blows, he jabbed his left at Hadden's jaw. But the nobleman pranced out of reach.

"I want to relish this," the earl said. "I want to whittle

you down, piece by piece, and hear your screams when I break both your arms."

"You sure do *talk* a good fight," Fargo remarked.

Hadden moved closer and twirled his hips. His right leg lashed out, then his left.

Fargo absorbed the brutal strikes with his forearms. He had been kicked by foes plenty of times, but not like this. Hadden gave a wicked snap to his legs that lent his kicks added power and caused excruciating torment.

Incensed, Hadden kicked faster and harder, battering Fargo backward until he was at the side of the wallow and had no farther to go. Hadden assumed a wide stance and paused. "Good reflexes alone won't save you."

Digging in the soles of his boots, Fargo tensed for the next onslaught. When it came, Hadden fought with cold fury, trying to break down his guard, those rock-hard hands and feet never still for a moment. One blow connected with Fargo's left elbow, and his arm immediately went numb from his fingertips to his shoulder.

Fargo retreated, backing up the short incline until he was higher than the earl, who tried to trip him. Dodging to the right, Fargo saw puffs of dust rise from under his feet, and acting on this observation he kicked at the dirt, dislodging clumps that rained down on Hadden. The Englishman swatted at them to keep the dirt from getting into his eyes. And all the while the dust grew thicker and thicker.

Hadden began coughing and tried to back out of the choking cloud, his gaze dropping to the ground.

Uncoiling, Fargo leaped, tackling the nobleman around the waist, his shoulder ramming into Hadden's gut as they crashed down at the bottom of the wallow. Hadden wrenched to the left and tried to throw Fargo off, but Fargo planted a right cross that rocked the earl and brought a drop of blood to the corner of his mouth.

Pushing to his knees, Fargo buried one fist in Hadden's stomach and drew back his other for the final blow. But Hadden, in desperation, drove a knifelike hand into Fargo's ribs.

Bolts of agony sheared through Fargo's torso. It felt as if a rib had been shattered, and he threw himself out of reach to pull himself together. A foot clipped him on the ear as he did.

Hadden was slow to rise. The drop of blood had become a trickle. Grime caked his sweaty face and neck and soiled his shirt. He drew himself up to his full height, then assumed one of those strange stances. "No one lays a finger on me, ever," he rasped.

Fargo licked his lips and raised his fists. He had barely set himself when Hadden came on like a whirlwind again. This time there was a difference, though. Where before the earl had aimed blows at Fargo's chest and belly, now the earl tried to connect with Fargo's throat and eyes. Hadden was trying to cripple him, and Fargo knew it.

Forced to give ground, Fargo nonetheless held his own and blocked most of the earl's efforts. He could tell that Hadden was tiring, that the heat was taking its toll. If he could hold out a while longer, Hadden would be at his mercy.

Thinking those thoughts, Fargo failed to pay attention to where he was going. Suddenly his left boot hit something and he lost his balance. A jarring kick, perfectly aimed, sprawled him on top of the thoroughbred, and as he propped both hands under himself to rise, another kick exploded against his temple and the whole wallow spun crazily.

Fargo felt a hand grip his buckskin shirt, felt himself being hauled into a sitting posture. Through a blurry veil he saw Hadden smirking at him, saw the nobleman's arm rise. And instinctively he snapped his leg up into Hadden's groin.

Sputtering, the earl released his hold and grabbed his privates. He staggered off, bellowing.

Fargo shook his head and shoved off the horse. He stalked the nobleman, his right fist clenched so hard it hurt, and when Hadden stopped and looked back, he plowed his knuckles into Hadden's mouth. The earl swayed on his heels but did not go down, which suited Fargo just fine. He put all he had into one more punch, and Ashley Hadden hit the ground in a heap.

Taking ragged breaths, Fargo shuffled to his hat, then to the Ovaro. He had to lift his leg twice before he hooked his boot in the stirrup. Pulling himself into the saddle, he sat looking down at the nobleman. "You're on your own, you son of a bitch," he said, and rode out of the wallow.

Fargo's body ached terribly; it felt as if he had run an Indian gauntlet. His mouth was puffy, his knuckles were split. He took off his bandanna and wiped his face and neck. Only once did he look back, and there was no sign of the Earl of Somerset.

Soon the sluggish breeze helped to revitalize him. Fargo cantered off in pursuit of the English party, constantly on the lookout for Eagle Claw and company. He figured he had half an hour of daylight left. After that he would have to watch for a campfire.

Although Fargo wanted to push straight on through until he overtook the wagon, he changed his plans when a small stand of trees reared to the south. Where there were trees, there was water. Once there, he searched diligently and found a damp area. Grabbing a broken limb, he dug, scraping at the soil until water seeped into the hole he had made.

The Ovaro bowed its head without any coaxing.

Taking off his hat, Fargo filled it with water, then upended it over his head. Rivulets seeped under his shirt and down his chest and back. Chuckling, he soaked his bandanna and tied it around his neck to keep him cool. A few sips of the muddy water were all he dared take before resuming his journey.

Twilight ruled the prairie, casting the waving grass in a gray shroud. Fargo spied deer far off, and the thought of roast venison made his stomach growl. But he left them alone. He dared not delay any longer, not with nine lives at stake.

Darkness gradually embraced the plain, and the moon rose to the east. Before long, the wolves and coyotes were in full chorus, seemingly vying with one another to see which could wail the loudest. Wavering howls and piercing yips came from all directions, and every so often mixed among them would be the throaty snarl of a cougar or the rumbling grunt of a prowling grizzly. These were all sounds Fargo knew well, and he was no more disturbed by them than a city dweller would be by the barking of dogs or the meowing of cats.

Several hours after sunset, Fargo finally spotted what he had sought, a small pinpoint of flickering light way off in the distance. Since Indians would never make a fire that could be seen from so far away, he knew it had to be the Britishers. Or else their burning wagon.

Fargo unlimbered the Sharps and fed in a cartridge, just to be on the safe side. He felt some of the tension drain from him when he drew close enough to see figures moving about, and relaxed completely when female laughter carried to his ears. He was fifty yards out when a familiar voice hailed him.

"Hold up there and identify yourself!"

"It's Fargo, Oakley."

"Come on in, then."

The small party gathered around as Fargo wearily slid from the saddle and looped the reins around a spoke in the rear wheel of the wagon. The question on their faces was obvious, a question Kendra Hadden put to words.

"You're alone? Where is the earl?"

"He should be along shortly," Fargo answered. He walked to the fire and helped himself to a steaming cup of coffee.

The Britons formed a circle around him, and the physician, Revis, cleared his throat. "Are we to understand you left the earl out there all alone in the middle of this godforsaken prairie?"

Fargo took a lusty swallow and smacked his lips. "Yes."

"Good God, Yank! Why?" Oakley asked.

"He didn't care much for my company," Fargo said, and tried to let it go at that.

Elizabeth Hadden stepped up to him to shake a crooked finger in his face. "How dare you, you barbarian! I insist that you get on that horse of yours and go find my brother this very instant!"

"Insist all you want," Fargo said. "But it's not going to happen. Your brother is a big boy. He can take care of himself." Touching his hat, he rose and walked to the rear of the wagon to be by himself. A shadow fell over him as he leaned on the wood panel and pushed back his hat.

"What happened out there?"

Fargo looked at Kendra. "Your husband thought he

could treat me like he does you and everyone else. He was wrong."

"Is he alive?"

"Do you care?"

The query caused Kendra to do a double take and place a pale hand to her alabaster throat. "That's a terrible thing to ask a married woman."

"You call what you have a marriage?"

Kendra took a step backward. "I'm shocked, Skye Fargo. I knew you were rough around the edges, but I didn't think you could be outright mean."

"I'm being no meaner than you are to yourself every day you stay with him," Fargo responded. "But don't worry. If he comes charging in here like I figure he will, your days of being beaten will be over."

"What do you mean?"

"I'm hoping he'll go for a gun or pull a knife," Fargo said. "Any excuse he gives me, the end result will be the same."

Her voice lowered to a whisper so none of the others could overhear. "You would do that for me?"

"There's only one way to deal with a mad dog," Fargo replied.

"Surely you must know nothing can come of it. No matter what happens between Ashley and you, no matter what feelings I might have, in the end I must return to England and you must go on with your own life."

"I wouldn't have it any other way."

Kendra came nearer and put her warm hand on his. "Then *why*? I must know. Is this strictly on my account?"

"No. Let's just say it's so I can look at myself in the mirror again, and drop the subject." Fargo reached up to stroke her cheek but she pulled away, turned on her heel, and fled to the security of the fire.

"Women!" Fargo muttered. He polished off his coffee, then spent the next half-hour stripping the Ovaro and giving the stallion a thorough rubdown with handfuls of grass. He was about done when Oakley approached.

"We've decided to go out after him if he's not back soon."

"Your choice," Fargo said.

"Will you go with us and guide us to where you last saw him?"

"No."

The bodyguard sighed. "Sometimes you make it hard for a bloke to like you, Yank. And I do, despite your behavior." He paused. "Granted the earl can be difficult at times, but you don't know him like we do. He does have his kind moments, and he's always considerate of his staff."

"I saw how considerate he was of Jeems."

"So Jeems had a whipping. He wasn't beaten that badly, and you can be damn sure he'll think twice before he takes liberties with one of the women again. A nasty thing like that has to be nipped in the bud at the outset. Don't you see?"

Fargo threw down the last handful of grass. "You're wasting your breath if you're trying to convince me the earl is a saint. I know better."

Their talk was ended by a hail from the northwest, and in short order Ashley Hadden rode into the firelight astride an Arapaho warhorse that had been ridden to the brink of lathered exhaustion. Immediately the members of his party gathered to pester him with questions and ask about his well-being. There were gasps of outrage when they saw his split lips and puffy mouth, and furious stares were directed at Fargo.

The earl noticed and said, "Don't blame the plainsman. Hasn't he told you about our clash with the Arapahos?"

Fargo listened to a brief account of the battle at the wallow that did not include any mention of his fight with the nobleman. Hadden explained their separation by saying the Indian horse had been too worn-out to go very fast, and that Hadden had insisted he ride on ahead to make sure the women were safe. When the earl was finished, the Britishers praised him as a hero.

Fargo did not try to set them straight. He knew that most of them would not believe him anyway. Gathering his saddle and bedroll, he moved off to sleep by himself and was spreading out his blankets when he heard footsteps and pivoted, his right hand dropping to the Colt.

Ashley Hadden gave an oily smile and held up his hands to show he was unarmed. "I wanted a few words with you."

"We have nothing left to say to one another."

"There you're wrong," the earl responded. He glanced over a shoulder to confirm no one was within earshot, then he said softly, "It would be best for all concerned if you do not tell anyone about our little fray. The others might hold it against you."

Fargo laughed and sat. "The only reason you don't want me to tell them is that you don't want them to know someone beat you fair and square."

Hadden forgot himself and raised his voice. "No one has ever beaten me, not in the long run." He leaned forward. "And one other thing. You are no longer welcome here. Tomorrow you will go your way and we will go ours."

"I'll leave when I'm ready and not before."

"We'll see about that." Wheeling, the earl stormed off.

Fargo propped himself on his saddle and stared thoughtfully out over the prairie. He had to admit that Hadden had surprised him. Given the nobleman's temperament, Fargo had reckoned on Hadden barreling into camp like a mad bull and taking up where they had left off at the wallow. But the earl had been remarkably levelheaded. Which in itself was suspicious.

Fargo had met men like the Earl of Somerset before, men who felt they had the God-given right to lord it over anyone and everyone, who had to have their own way no matter how much suffering they caused. They did not take being beaten graciously. Hadden would want revenge, but he would not challenge Fargo face-to-face. No, the earl would concoct a devious scheme of some sort. So Fargo had to stay on his guard every minute of every day.

The big man lay down and cradled the back of his head in his hands. If he had any sense, he mentally noted, he would ride on out in the morning. But he couldn't very well desert the women, not when they needed him to help get them safely to Kansas City. Whether Hadden liked it or not, he was staying. And if the earl raised a stink or threw another one of those fancy kicks at him, he was going to break every bone in the bastard's body.

Soon Fargo was asleep. As always he slept lightly, so when he heard the near-silent tread of someone creeping toward him, he was instantly awake, his hand on the Colt. He caught a whiff of perfume as he sat up, and a soft hand covered his mouth.

"Shhhhh. Don't make any noise," Kendra Hadden whispered. "We must talk."

Fargo nodded and checked on the others. Every last one was sound asleep, even Jeems, who was supposed to be on guard duty but had dozed off seated near the fire.

Kendra took his hand, and together they moved out of the firelight and a dozen yards from the camp. She stopped and turned toward him, her face inches from his, her warm breath fluttering on his mouth.

Fargo breathed in her scent and felt the warmth given off by her voluptuous body. Being so close to her made his loins twitch. He had to rein in his desire or he would have taken her then and there. "What is it?" he asked quietly.

The countess looked down and wrung her hands. "I'd like you to leave in the morning."

"No, you don't mean that."

Kendra glanced up, her features exquisitely lovely in the moonlight. "You are the most exasperating man I've ever met. How can you stand there and presume to tell me what I really want and don't want?"

"There's only one thing you really want."

"Oh. And what might that be?"

Fargo gently embraced her, meeting with no resistance. He lowered his lips to hers, felt them yield to his pressure and part to admit his tongue. A soft moan welled up in her throat and she went slack in his arms, as if overcome. When he pulled away, she took a deep breath and trembled.

"You are positively awful, taking advantage of me the way you do."

Again Fargo bent his mouth to hers. This time his hand roved to her shapely buttocks and he kneaded them, causing her hips to grind against his, lightly at first but then with increasing passion. At length he paused, but she clung to him, her cheek on his chest.

"You make me dizzy."

Fargo stroked her luxurious hair. "Why did you ask me to leave just now?"

"I don't care to see you hurt."

"Your husband?"

Kendra bobbed her head. "He won't tell me what happened out there today, but I know he is burning inside with a terrible rage. He wants you dead, Skye, and he'll stop at nothing to bring it about." She tilted her head to gaze fondly up at him. "All evening he dropped hints about how he is going to make you pay."

"He'll try," Fargo said.

Kendra pecked him on the chin and traced the outline of his jaw with her fingernail. "Sometimes I wish you had never come along. And at other times, I sit and dream of what it would be like to make love to you."

"You can do more than dream," Fargo said, joining their bodies once again. As his tongue entwined with hers, his hands drifted to her straining bosom and squeezed her twin globes. She wriggled and cooed and tried to suck his tongue down her throat.

Fargo ran a palm over her flat stomach to the junction of her thighs. He could feel the heat of her womanhood through the material of her dress, and when he pressed on her nether mound, she mashed into him so hard she nearly knocked him over. Breaking the kiss, she bit his neck, his lower lip, his earlobe. Her hands explored him from his chest to his waist but stopped short of his groin.

"I can't!" Kendra said, suddenly pulling away. "I took a vow to be true to Ashley."

"He doesn't love you," Fargo said, and kissed her on the forehead.

"It's not the man that's important. It's my vow."

Fargo clasped her waist and tried to pull her close.

"No!" Kendra whispered. "Please." She put a hand out to keep him from hugging her. "As much as I want to, I must remember my station."

"You're making a mistake."

"I know. But it can't be helped." Kendra tenderly stroked his face. "In the short time I've known you, I've come to learn that you are a man of your word. When you say you will do something, you do it. True?"

"In the West a man is only as good as his word."

"As that may be. You are a man of principle, whether you are willing to admit it or not. If you weren't, I wouldn't like you as much as I do." Kendra paused. "You must be true to your word and I must be true to mine. So long as I am Ashley's wife, I will give myself only to him." She gave him a quick kiss and hastened off.

Skye Fargo watched her go with mixed feelings. On the one hand he admired her honesty and character, on the other he wished she wasn't quite so almighty noble. He realized again that he might be wasting his time, but he was more determined than ever to stay with the party and see the journey through to its end. Come what may.

11

No one could ever accuse Ashley Hadden of being predictable. He had given Fargo an ultimatum, but the next morning he did not bring it up even once. Instead he ignored Fargo, as he prepared to go out after his bull yet again, this time with Hollis.

The sun had not yet cleared the horizon when the two men departed. Oakley was left in charge and soon had the rest of the party on the move. Elizabeth Hadden rode on the wagon beside the driver; Kendra and Flora rode side by side.

Fargo rode up to the bodyguard to announce, "I'm going to make a sweep of the countryside for a sign of the Arapahos. I should rejoin you about noon."

"Do what you want," Oakley said coldly.

"Is something wrong?" Fargo asked.

"You don't confide your secrets, I don't confide mine." Oakley slapped his heels against his horse and moved closer to the women.

Puzzled by the odd comment and the drastic change in the bodyguard's attitude, Fargo trotted northward. Of them all, Oakley had been one of the friendliest. Fargo couldn't understand what he had done to turn the man against him so suddenly. Shrugging, he passed it off as yet another quirk of the English.

For the next several hours Fargo hunted for signs of Eagle Claw's band. He saw plenty of wildlife but not a trace of the Arapahos—not so much as a single track.

Then, to Fargo's surprise, he came upon a long, low basin he had not known existed in that area. It contained a large inviting spring, and was lush with trees and undergrowth. From the rim of the flatland he looked down in wonder, observing white-tailed deer drinking water. They scattered as he galloped down into their isolated retreat.

Right away Fargo found tracks, the hoofprints of unshod horses. Close to the spring he also found the charred remains of a small fire. This had been where Eagle Claw camped for at least two days, judging by the sign. Fargo dug down in the fire with a stick and determined the bottom was still warm. Eagle Claw had left that very morning.

Fargo was relieved to find the tracks led off to the northwest, away from the earl's party. He decided to rest a spell and let the Ovaro drink while slaking his own thirst. As he raised his head from the delicious water, he was confounded to see Oakley riding into the basin at the exact same point he had.

Standing, Fargo waited for the Englishman. He wondered if maybe Eagle Claw had doubled back and attacked the group, for he could think of no other reason the bodyguard would leave the women and the wounded.

"I've never met anyone who can cover so much territory in so short a time, Yank," Oakley commented as he reined up. Taking off his hat, he ran a hand over his short hair. "I was hard-pressed to keep up with you."

"You've been following me since I left?" Fargo asked.

"Shortly after," Oakley amended.

"Why?"

"So we could have a chat," Oakley said. He began to put his hat back on, but as it rose even with his right shoulder he suddenly streaked a hand under his jacket and brought it out holding a Tranter. Pointing the gun, he said, "This is hard enough as it is. I would be grateful if you would do as I tell you without giving me an excuse to shoot."

"What the hell!" Fargo blurted, taking a step. He turned to stone upon hearing the click of the Tranter's hammer being pulled back.

"I mean it, Yank," Oakley warned. "I'll kill you if you give me cause."

Fargo held still while the Englishman dismounted. He didn't doubt for a moment that the bodyguard meant every word. Never once did the revolver barrel stray from his person. "Mind telling me what this is all about?" he asked, stalling in the hope Oakley would drop his guard.

"Don't play the innocent. I won't fall for it."

"The earl is behind this, isn't he? He sent you to kill me in his stead."

"How insulting. I'm his bodyguard, not a bloody murderer." Oakley sidled over to the spring and squatted to dip his other hand in the water. He took a sip, then said, "No, the earl is as much to blame for this as you are, but he didn't send me."

"Is it over Roberts?"

"I don't hold that against you. I would have done the same if he had been trying to kill me." Oakley's eyes narrowed. "You really don't know, do you? Strange. She claimed you did."

"Kendra?"

"Elizabeth."

The revelation made Fargo more confused than ever. "The earl's sister? I've never done anything to her. Why would she want me dead?"

Oakley moved to a log and took a seat. He transferred the Tranter to his left hand and remarked, "My shoulder is still sore from that bullet, but it's mending faster than I would have believed possible. What is it about the air out here?" He wagged the pistol. "I'll answer your question, but first unbuckle your gun belt and let it drop."

Frowning, Fargo did as instructed.

"Now reach down and take that nasty knife of yours and set it aside. And please do it slowly, or else."

The Arkansas toothpick was placed on the grass and Fargo straightened.

"Thank you. I can breathe a bit easier." Oakley stood and began talking, and as he talked, he idly paced back and forth. "I know that you colonial sorts do things differently in this country, and that you don't have royalty like we do in England. But I would have thought you'd have the good sense not to trifle with a married woman, and a countess at that."

"What difference does that make?"

"All the difference in the world, Yank. Kendra Hadden is a lady, and as such she's to be treated differently than you'd treat, say, Flora." Oakley paused. "And you must understand how we English feel about our royalty. They're very special, very dear to our hearts. We don't like to see them caught up in any kind of scandal. Proper image, and all that."

"I don't see what this has to do with me."

"I'm getting to that." The bodyguard sat down again. "You're well aware, I would imagine, that the earl and the countess are unhappy together. It's reached a point where the earl is considering divorce, despite the uproar that would cause and the shame it would bring to the Hadden family."

Fargo still had no idea where this train thought was leading, and he mentioned as much.

"You haven't guessed? The earl needs firm grounds to file for divorce, and what better grounds than his wife sleeping with another man? A while back he confided in his sister that he was going to encourage the two of you to, shall we say, get together. Later he would use Kendra's dalliance against her."

The news explained why the earl had been so friendly for a while. Fargo folded his arms, boiling with anger at being used as a puppet.

"Naturally, Elizabeth was horrified by the earl's plan. She didn't want her family name dragged through the mud. So she confided in Moulton, who so mysteriously vanished, and in Roberts, whom you killed. She convinced them that the best way to avoid scandal was to remove Kendra's temptation."

"Me," Fargo said.

"You."

At last the mystery had been cleared up, and Fargo knew whom to blame. "And now she's convinced you to take up where they left off?"

"Not quite, Yank," Oakley said. "I told you I'm not a murderer. So I came up with a better idea." Rising, he motioned for Fargo to back up, and after Fargo complied, he came forward to claim the gun belt and the toothpick. "So far Kendra has not had a chance to give in to her desire. And if we can keep you away from her until we reach Kansas City, she never will."

"You aim to leave me out here on foot," Fargo guessed.

Oakley nodded. "If it seems harsh, bear in mind that Elizabeth wanted me to shoot you down like a dog. Begged me, she did, with tears in her eyes." He backed up to his thoroughbred, the Tranter leveled. "Try not to hold this against me. I'm just doing what I think is best."

"It's no excuse. Leaving a man afoot is the same as signing his death warrant."

"Other men, yes. Not you. You're too tough to die."

Fargo had to stand there as the bodyguard mounted and then moved over to grasp the Ovaro's reins. "I'll be coming for my guns, Oakley."

"You'll find them at the Fairmont Hotel in Kansas City. We'll stay there a few days before heading east." Oakley waved the Tranter and was off, leading the pinto. He kept one eye trained over his shoulder until he reached the top of the basin. There he paused, raised an arm in salute, and galloped across the plain.

Fargo was fit to be tied. He took a few impulsive steps, then stopped, realizing he had no hope of overtaking the Britishers, even if he hiked the rest of the day and all night besides. He was stranded without a weapon in the heart of the prairie, alone without a horse in the middle of a land overrun with hostiles. It was what every frontiersman dreaded, a nightmare come true. But the situation could have been much worse. He had water, and there was game in the brush. He wouldn't die of thirst and he'd eat, at least until he set out across the prairie.

Not wasting any time, Fargo searched among the rocks bordering the spring till he located a flat one with a tapered edge. This he used to chop off a long, slender limb, and to sharpen the end of the limb until he had a suitable point.

Next Fargo found a shorter, stouter branch. He trimmed off the shoots, then split the top to form a crack that would hold the stone in place once he had wedged it down. From his buckskin shirt he plucked several whangs, and these he tied into one long makeshift cord of sufficient length to secure the stone to the limb. The end result was a heavy stone ax.

Fargo tucked the ax under his belt and went in search of his next meal. The deer were deep in the thickets, so he settled for something smaller, a rabbit that made the mistake of staring at him instead of fleeing. From ten feet away Fargo hurled his crude spear. He would have missed had the rabbit not taken a hop, right into the spear's path.

Pleased with himself, Fargo strolled back to the spring.

He was winding through the brush and had spotted the shimmering water just ahead when the quiet was broken by the drumming of hooves. Thinking that Oakley might have changed his mind and returned, Fargo dashed forward. Just in time he saw the band of Indians.

Ducking, Fargo scrambled into the undergrowth and dropped to his belly at the base of a bush. Once the warriors were close enough, he recognized Eagle Claw among them. He counted nine riders, not eight, which mystified him until he was startled to identify the ninth rider as Hollis, the second manservant who had gone off that morning with the earl.

Fargo held his spear in front of him as the Arapahos slowed to a stop and swung to the ground. They were in fine spirits, smiling and gesturing often at their glum prisoner. Hollis was bound at the wrists. He'd been beaten, as his split cheek and bloody mouth testified. He had the look of a condemned man, and whenever one of the warriors came near him, he cringed in fear.

The unforeseen return of the war party put Fargo in an awkward position. He wanted to help the Englishman. He knew the fate in store for him, but there was nothing he could do, not outnumbered as he was. Not without his guns.

The Arapahos were so excited about the capture of the white-eye that not one of them thought to check the ground for new tracks, and in no time their mounts had wiped out the prints made by the Ovaro and the thoroughbred.

Fargo tried to catch the drift of their talk, but he did not speak Arapaho. He had to lie there as Hollis was hauled from his horse and thrown roughly to the ground near the spring. Several of the warriors took turns kicking and slapping him, laughing when he groveled. They weren't being cruel. They were testing him, gauging his courage by how well he held up. When he showed that he had none, they showed their scorn.

Eagle Claw barked orders. Hollis was hauled to a nearby tree and lashed to the trunk. The horses were watered while the warriors devoted themselves to sharpening their knives and tomahawks. A heated dispute broke out when Eagle Claw pointed at another of the braves, and the man responded with angry words and motions.

Fargo wondered what it was all about and presently had

an answer. Eagle Claw and all the warriors except the one picked mounted their horses. In a flurry of dust they galloped to the south, leaving their fuming companion behind to guard the Englishman.

It did not take a Pinkerton detective to figure out where the band was headed. Worry gnawed at Fargo as he watched the cloud of dust recede in the distance. Before sundown the Arapahos would catch up with the earl's party; by nightfall every last one would be dead. Except the women. The Arapahos would have another fate in store for them.

Fargo stared at the two horses grazing close to the spring. He had to reach them, and quickly. But first he had to deal with the lone warrior who was gathering wood for a fire. Getting close enough to use his spear would be a problem, since there was no cover near the opposite side of the spring. And he didn't dare miss. The warrior had a bow and a quiver full of arrows.

The Arapaho finished collecting wood but made no attempt to get a fire going. Bow and arrow in hand, he walked over to Hollis and began taunting the Englishman by poking the arrow into Hollis's legs. Every time Hollis yelped, the warrior roared. His back was to the spring.

Fargo left the rabbit lying beside the brush and crawled toward the water. He had an idea how the could get to the far side without being seen, but a lot depended on his timing. Under the low branch of a tree that overhung the spring, he stopped and took off his hat. The warrior was still having a grand time with Hollis.

Slowly Fargo eased into the water, being careful not to splash or create big ripples. The spring was twenty feet across and at least eight feet deep, so it was simple to sink below the surface and swim underwater. He stroked at a crawl, barely moving his arms and legs in order to avoid making a disturbance the Arapaho might notice. In his right hand he held his spear.

Fargo coasted to a halt a few feet from the west side. The natural bowl had been carved from solid rock, and there were ample handholds for him to use while treading water. Above him sunlight dappled the surface. Satisfied it was safe, he was about to venture to the top when a shadow played over the water.

A distorted figure appeared, standing at the edge of the spring. The warrior was gazing eastward, his shaft notched to his sinew bowstring.

Fargo did not move a muscle. He knew if the Arapaho glanced down he was done for. Seconds crawled by and his lungs started to ache. The pain grew and grew, racking his chest with torment. He did not know how much longer he could hold his breath. His lungs were close to bursting.

Fargo had no choice. He had to surface, and as he firmed his grip on the spear and tensed his legs to push off from the rock wall, he saw the Arapaho lower the bow and kneel to take a drink. The warrior kept staring suspiciously at the vegetation as he was bending over. Not until his face was inches from the water did he look down, blink in astonishment, and try to push back.

Hurtling upward, Fargo cleaved the water smoothly, gripping the shaft of the spear in both hands as he exploded from the spring in a geyser of water. The sharp tip caught the brave under the jawbone and ripped into the soft flesh, impaling him.

Fargo's momentum gave him the extra force needed to shove the Arapaho backward. The brave stumbled and fell, clutching at the spear. Fargo let go, gripped the slippery rim, and pulled himself out, rolling as he came over the side. Rising, he streaked the stone ax from under his belt and shot it overhead.

The Arapaho had wrenched the spear free and was convulsing in a pool of blood. He tried to stand, to draw his knife.

A single stroke of the ax was all it took and the warrior fell flat, lifeless. Fargo took deep breaths, filling his heaving lungs, and turned.

Hollis was flabbergasted by the turn of events. He gawked at the big man in buckskins, his wounds forgotten.

Fargo took the warrior's knife and hurried over. "Can you ride?" he asked.

The Englishman simply gaped.

"Are you fit to sit a saddle?" Fargo demanded, slicing into the coils of rope.

"Where? How? What—?" Hollis blurted.

Fargo grabbed the front of the Englishman's shirt and gave him a violent shake. "Snap out of it! We have to reach the others before the Arapaho wipe them out." He resumed cutting the bonds. "Can you ride?"

"Ride? Yes, you bloody well bet I can ride," Hollis said, regaining some of his composure. He heaved against the rope, anxious to be loose, and when the last strand parted and his wrists were no longer tied, he turned and placed a hand on Fargo's shoulder. "I can never thank you enough, mate. And to think I didn't like you very much before this."

"Right now we have the rest of your party to think of," Fargo said, moving around the spring. In no time he had retrieved his hat and was slowly approaching the two horses so as not to scare them off. The thoroughbred allowed him to walk right up, but the warhorse acted skittish until a few soft words and a few strokes of its neck quieted it down.

Before mounting, Fargo slung the warrior's quiver over his back and the bow over his shoulder. He swung onto the warhorse, waited while Hollis climbed on the thoroughbred, and headed out at a gallop.

"Where the devil did you come from?" the Englishman wanted to know.

"It's a long story," Fargo said, and that was all he would say on the subject. Revealing the truth might only serve to turn Hollis against him, and he had enough to handle as it was. "What about you? Where's the earl?"

"Dead."

Fargo glanced at him. "You're sure?"

"As sure as I can be," Hollis answered. "We were after that damn silly buffalo of his when the red demons came charging out of nowhere. I was caught before I could go ten meters, but the earl led five of them on a merry chase. They all rode out of sight over a rise, and five minutes later the Indians returned alone, smiling and joking."

"So you didn't see Hadden die with your own eyes?"

"Well, no."

"Did you see any of the Arapahos with a fresh scalp?"

"No, but I wasn't actually looking for one. I was too worried about my own hair."

"How far from the camp had you gone when you were jumped?"

"I wouldn't know," Hollis said. "I'm not much good at

guessing distances, but I'd say we had been riding for three or four hours."

"They took you straight to the spring?"

"That they did, although they did stop once when one of them found some ruts. That made the whole bunch as excited as fishmongers when the boats come in."

Fargo nodded. The Arapahos had stumbled on the tracks of the wagon. Small wonder Eagle Claw had been in such a hurry to go after the Britons; there were scalps to be taken, coups to be performed, and booty to be hauled back to the village.

Hollis goaded his mount to go faster so he could stay abreast of Fargo. "There's something else I have to say," he remarked, speaking loudly to be heard over the pounding of hooves. "It's the least I can do after all you've done."

"You don't owe me anything," Fargo said.

"Wrong, mate." Hollis tightened his hold on his reins. He was a poor rider, as the wild flapping of his arms and legs showed. "It's clear to me that you're not as bad a bloke as the earl made you out to be. He went on and on this morning about how you were pure scum, and how he wanted to teach you a few things."

"What did he have in mind?"

"He was planning to get the lot of us men to jump you tonight when you weren't looking. He had it in mind to whip you and then leave you behind."

"Birds of a feather," Fargo muttered to himself.

"What?"

"Nothing."

"I just thought you should know. If by some miracle he does show up and tries to go through with it, I won't join in." Hollis paused. "I know I shouldn't betray his trust, but I have to be true to my own principles."

"Consider us even," Fargo said, and returned the Englishman's smile.

In silence they rode on, pushing their mounts to the limits of endurance regardless of the heat and the distance they had to cover. Fargo's keen eyes were the first to spot the three large black birds circling on the horizon.

"What are those?" Hollis asked moments later.

"Buzzards."

12

It was Oakley.

They found the bodyguard on his back, five arrows jutting from his stomach and chest. His scalp had been lifted, an ear chopped off, and his eyes gouged out.

Fargo dismounted and read the sign to get the whole story. Either Oakley had been taking his sweet time getting back to the wagon, or more likely, the Ovaro had been giving him trouble, balking and slowing him down. In any event, the Arapahos had caught him in the open and there had been a running fight. One of the arrows had brought Oakley low, and although he had emptied his Tranter, the Arapahos had made a pincushion of him and taken his hair while he still lived. His death had been horribly slow and painful.

"Say! Look over there!" Hollis suddenly cried.

Fargo looked and was happy to see the Ovaro trotting toward him. The Pinto had run off during the fight and no doubt outdistanced any of the warriors foolish enough to try to catch him.

"Isn't he yours?" Hollis asked.

"Sure is," Fargo said with pride. When the stallion reached him, he draped an arm over its neck and scratched behind its ears. Then keenly aware they were losing precious time, he went to climb up, stopping in delight when he found his gun belt hanging from the saddle horn and his Sharps in the scabbard. Discarding the bow and quiver, he strapped on the Colt, checked the rifle, and mounted.

"What about the Indian pony?" the Englishman inquired.

"It can fend for itself," Fargo said.

"And Oakley? Shouldn't we bury him?"

Fargo glanced overhead where there were now five buzzards. "We'll let nature take its course." He headed out. "If we don't get a move on, there will be a lot more who need burying."

Southward the two men flew. An hour later Fargo was again the first to spy a grayish-black smudge marring the bright-blue vault of the sky.

Hollis pointed and asked, "Is that what I think it is?"

"Smoke," Fargo confirmed.

The English had fought bravely, but the four men and three women had been no match for the wily, lightning-quick Arapahos. Apparently they had stopped the wagon and taken shelter under it. Their horses had been promptly driven off. Then the Arapahos had circled, drawing closer and closer while pouring arrows into the van and those hiding underneath it.

Fargo uncovered the bodies of the sawbones, Jeems, and one other man in the burning ruin of the wagon. The fourth man, Williams, had tried to run off but had not made it very far with his broken leg. A lance had brought him low, and he had been finished off with a tomahawk blow to the skull.

Hollis had tears in his eyes as he surveyed the slaughter. "Bloody hell!" he repeated, over and over, wandering about like one stripped of his reason.

Fargo devoted himself to unraveling details of the attack. He discovered a bloody spot in the grass where one of the Arapahos had fallen, but could not determine whether the man had lived or died. The warriors had taken everything they wanted from the wagon before setting it alight. With their plunder lashed to some of the stolen horses, they had ridden to the southwest.

"What about the women?" Hollis questioned, his voice cracking from the strain.

"Prisoners," Fargo said.

"All three?"

"Near as I can tell."

"Oh God!" Hollis wailed. "You don't think the savages have already—" He stopped, unable to complete the thought.

"Not yet," Fargo said, rising from the tracks he had been examining. "Tonight, maybe. Or the warriors might decide to take them as wives, in which case they'll wait until they reach their village."

"We have to go after them!"

Fargo snatched the Englishman's sleeve to prevent Hollis from running off. "I'm the one who has to go. You stay here and give your friends a decent burial."

"What chance do you stand alone?"

"A better one than if I have to watch out for you, too," Fargo said. "I've fought Indians before. I know what to expect. You don't."

"I don't like the idea of being all alone. I won't last long out here."

Fargo stepped to the Ovaro, opened a saddlebag, and took out enough jerky to last several days. As he was pulling his hand out he bumped a hard object that nicked his finger, and rising on tiptoe he peered inside and saw the Arkansas toothpick. He slid the knife into his ankle sheath without delay, then gave the jerky to Hollis.

"But what about water? I might die of thirst before you get back."

"In the morning the grass will be covered with dew. Tear off part of your sleeve, soak it in the dew, and wring it out over your mouth." Fargo strode to the pinto and forked leather. "It won't be much but it will keep you alive."

Hollis had one last objection. "I don't have a gun. How am I supposed to protect myself?"

"I can't lend you one of mine," Fargo said. "I'll need them both." He nodded at the thoroughbred. "Keep your horse close, and if you see Indians coming, head southeast. In two days or so you'll come on a wagon trail that will take you east all the way to Fort Leavenworth."

"Two days?" Hollis repeated with interest.

Fargo turned the stallion and looked over his shoulder. "If you build a fire, keep it as small as you can. And it might help if you can get your horse to lie down so no one can spot it from far off."

"I'll do my best, sir."

"Good luck," Fargo said. He trotted out on the trail of the band, marking the position of the sun. Eagle Claw would be unable to make good time with the three women and a small herd of horses to look after, so Fargo counted on overtaking them shortly after dark. That would be the easy part. Rescuing the women without getting any of them killed would be a lot harder.

The sun gradually dipped toward the skyline. Fargo was alert in case the Arapahos stopped sooner than he figured. The tracks and droppings told him he was getting closer by the minute, and every so often he would rise in the stirrups to survey the plain.

A loud whinny gave the Arapahos away. On hearing it, Fargo reined up and jumped down so his silhouette could not be seen from a distance. Ground-hitching the pinto, he cat-footed forward with the Sharps in hand until he came to the top of a dry wash. Low voices reached his ears, mixed with the sound of milling horses.

Fargo crawled the last few yards. From his vantage point he could see the Arapahos camped thirty yards to his right at a point where the wash widened. The thoroughbreds had been herded into a small nook and the nook closed off with piled brush and tumbleweeds. A fire had been built, and seated around it talking were five warriors. The body of a sixth lay nearby, covered with a buffalo robe. The women were off by themselves, Elizabeth and Flora showing their fear in the looks they cast at the Indians, Kendra as self-possessed as always.

Eagle Claw and his men were in a good mood despite the loss of their fellows. They had taken two small bottles of liquor from the wagon and were passing it around.

Fargo knew enough of Indian ways to know they would stay up late swapping stories. How much they drank and whether or not they posted a guard would determine whether he could rescue the women anytime soon. He stared at one of the warriors, who had two scalps hanging from his belt, and abruptly realized there was a brave missing.

Fargo tallied them up. There had been sixteen initially. He'd killed the two sent to keep watch on the Britons, and later six more had been slain during the fight at the buffalo wallow. Another had died at the spring. There should be seven left, but there were only six, counting the dead one. Where was the last warrior?

Fargo had a hunch, and it made him ill at ease. The seventh brave had probably gone to the spring to bring back Hollis and the warrior left to watch him. Once the brave learned the truth, he would fly to the wash to inform Eagle Claw. And that meant he would arrive sometime during the night.

Fargo had to be careful he wasn't spotted. And he had to hide the Ovaro. Snaking backward, he stood and hastened to the pinto, leading it south along the twists and turns of the wash until he came to a buckled spot where he could descend without making noise. Once the stallion was secreted, he climbed the west side and crept northward.

Fargo worked his way to a mesquite bush perched on the rim above the horses. He had no sooner taken up position than one of the warriors stood and walked over to the women. Flora and Elizabeth recoiled, but Kendra held her chin high. The warrior studied them, then seized Elizabeth and dragged her toward the fire.

The earl's sister put up quite a fight, kicking and clawing like a wildcat. The warrior stopped and cuffed her when she scratched his leg open. She sagged now, cowering as he pulled her the rest of the way and then unceremoniously flung her to the dirt next to Eagle Claw.

Fargo pressed the Sharps to his shoulder. As much as he disliked Elizabeth Hadden, and despite her attempts to have him rubbed out, he couldn't lie there and do nothing while she was violated. He aimed at Eagle Claw but held his fire, waiting to see what would happen.

Elizabeth sat up, glaring at her captors. She regained some of her old spunk and declared, "What do you heathens intend doing with us?"

Eagle Claw said something that made the warriors laugh.

"I'll have you know I'm sister to the Earl of Somerset," Elizabeth declared. "Harm me, and the full might of the British Empire will be turned against you and your tribe. You will be exterminated to the last man."

The warrior who had dragged her over suddenly reached out, grabbed her by the front of her dress, and yanked. Buttons popped, bows ripped, and her dress was torn open from her throat to her waist, exposing her undergarments.

Elizabeth squawked while frantically trying to cover herself. She slapped at the warrior, crying, "How dare you, you filthy beast! I'll see that you pay for this outrage!"

The warrior struck her on the chin, knocking her down. He stood over her, leering, and bent to lift the hem of her dress.

Fargo had touched his cheek to the Sharps and was curling back the hammer when out of the corner of his eye he saw Kendra Hadden advancing with her fists clenched. Before the Arapahos became aware of her, she gave the leering warrior a shove that sent him stumbling into the fire. The warrior yelled in anger and jumped clear, slapping at flames that licked at his moccasins. Eagle Claw and the rest thought his antics were hilarious.

Kendra, meanwhile, had braced her hands under Elizabeth's arms and lifted. With one arm draped protectively over Elizabeth's shoulder, Kendra began backing away from the brave.

The warrior she had pushed was not about to let her leave. Out flashed his knife. Inflamed at being put to shame, he raised it for a killing stroke.

Fargo shifted the Sharps and took a quick bead. His finger had just touched the trigger when there arose the sound of rapid hoofbeats, and a warrior astride a sorrel galloped down the wash into the firelight.

The Arapahos were on their feet in an instant. They gathered close as the rider vaulted off his mount and went on at length in an agitated manner.

Fargo could guess the identity of the newcomer. The brave's timely arrival had caused the rest to forget all about Kendra and Elizabeth, and the countess lost no time in taking the earl's sister over to where Flora sat. Fargo lowered the Sharps and awaited developments. He did not have to wait very long.

Eagle Claw and three other warriors ran to their horses. The brave sent to the spring remounted. In short order they were racing to the northeast, leaving two men behind to guard the women and the thoroughbreds.

Fargo liked the new odds. He rested his chin on his forearms, in no hurry to move in since it would take Eagle Claw most of the night to reach the basin and return. The women were being ignored, so they were safe for a while, and that was all that concerned him.

The two warriors huddled at the fire until close to midnight. The flames had dwindled low when the taller of the pair picked up a rifle, the shorter a rope, and they both stepped over to the captives.

"I won't let you tie me!" Elizabeth declared.

"Hush," Kendra said. "Didn't you learn anything earlier? We don't want to make them mad."

Elizabeth refused to be cowed. "I will not submit to the sort of treatment reserved for common criminals!" She drew away as the short warrior reached for her, and was slammed onto her back and pinned.

Kendra and Flora moved to her aid but halted at a harsh word from the tall brave, who covered them with the rifle. In their turn, they were bound hand and foot and left lying in the dirt."

"Animals!" Elizabeth snapped as the Arapahos walked off. "Wait until the English ambassador hears of this outrage!"

The tall warrior raised his right fist to his forehead, his knuckles pointed outward, and moving his hand to the left, made a small circle. At this the short warrior chuckled.

So did Skye Fargo. The gesture had been sign language for "brain in a whirl," which was as good a description of the snotty blue-blood as anyone was likely to make.

Elizabeth could not leave well-enough alone. She managed to sit up and shouted shrilly, "I can't wait for my brother to get here! He'll whip you within an inch of your miserable lives, you smelly sons of bitches!"

"Please be quiet," Kendra said.

"Like hell I will," Elizabeth responded. Beside herself, she tugged at her ropes, puffing and muttering. On failing to loosen them, she shoved to her knees and screeched, "I can't stand being tied! Release me at once, damn you!"

There was no warning for what came next. The tall warrior simply turned and fired, his shot striking the earl's sister full in the face and flipping her rearward. Kendra and Flora screamed, cries they choked off when the tall warrior swung the rifle toward them.

Fargo squatted and brought up the Sharps, but the tall

135

warrior turned back to the fire and sat down. The short one came toward the horses to check on them. Fargo had to resist an urge to open fire, since there was a slim chance the tall one might get off a shot or two before he dropped, and out of spite he might shoot the women.

The short brave walked along the brush barrier, testing it in spots, then strolled to the fire. Evidently neither of them intended to sleep anytime soon, as they each took turns tipping a bottle to their lips while making small talk.

Fargo did not move a muscle until the warriors had drained every last drop of liquor. By then the short one was acting tipsy and the tall one had stretched out on his back. Moving to the edge, Fargo studied the wash, seeking the best way down. Most of the horses were dozing, a few nibbling on scattered bunches of grass. Kendra and Flora were on their sides, facing one another, their faces lost in inky shadow. He could not tell whether they were awake or not, but he doubted they could sleep under the circumstances.

Fargo had two choices. He could skirt the horses, sneak to the bottom, and work his way close enough to make certain he killed the braves with one shot apiece, but in doing so he must cross two open areas and might be spotted. Or he could go straight over the side, down into the stolen herd, and then pick his way through them to the brush barrier, which lay within fifteen feet of the fire. There would be more cover but also more risk, for all it would take was one skittish horse to give him away.

Fargo chose the second way. Crawling to the edge, he cautiously lowered his legs over the side and found a purchase on the steep slope. Scrub bushes clung to the wash wall, their roots so firmly embedded that Fargo used them to clamber safely to the bottom.

The thoroughbreds nearest the side had brought their heads up and were staring at him intently, unsure of whether he posed a threat.

Fargo tiptoed to the closest horse and patted its chest, whispering, "Don't any of you make any noise or I'm a goner."

His tone and actions reassured them and most went back to dozing. He advanced slowly, hunched low, avoiding horses that acted the least bit nervous, stroking those he brushed against to calm them.

Halfway to the barrier Fargo ran into a problem. A gelding in front of him gave a low snort and pounded the ground with one hoof. Fargo halted, counting on the horse to soon lose interest and move off. But the contrary gelding came nearer instead, its nostrils wide, its head bobbing in agitation.

"Easy, boy," Fargo whispered. "You don't need to be scared of me."

The gelding stopped, cocked an eye at him, and snorted again, only much louder this time.

Fargo glanced at the Arapahos. The short one was poking a branch into the fire. The tall one had sat up and was gazing at the herd. Tense seconds passed, then the tall warrior sank back down, satisfied all was well.

The gelding was holding its ground. It took a few more steps and pawed the ground several more times, its tail flicking.

Fargo knew the signs. The horse would either rear and try to crush him with its hooves or it would dash off among the other animals, making a ruckus that would bring the Arapahos on the run. He had to soothe it somehow. Yet if he reached out, the gelding might take that as a threatening gesture and all hell would break loose.

A mare standing quietly nearby offered Fargo the means to avoid a clash. Keeping his eyes on the gelding, he sidled over to her and rubbed her side, then slipped underneath her and crouched. She lifted a back leg and stamped, so he softly patted her belly.

The gelding suddenly came toward the mare. From where Fargo squatted, all he could see was its legs. Unsure of what it was up to, he backed up, to the opposite side of the mare. The gelding stopped and Fargo saw its nose appear below the mare's flank. Its nostrils flaring, the gelding sniffed and sniffed, apparently in an effort to get his scent.

Fargo hoped the mare wouldn't move. He stroked her while holding onto her rear leg. After a minute the gelding stopped sniffing and walked off, so Fargo slid out and stood. His elbow against her shoulder, he grasped her mane and guided her toward the barrier, using her to shield him from the gelding. She docilely went along.

At the barrier Fargo released her and sank to his knees. He peeked over the top, noting that neither of the women had moved, and faced the fire. The tall warrior was still lying down, but the short one had disappeared!

Confounded, Fargo looked in all directions. He had to know where the brave had gotten to. There was no movement anywhere, and he was beginning to think the warrior had gone off to sleep alone when brush rustled to the south and the short Arapaho appeared, hitching at his leggings.

Fargo hunkered down, listening to the brave's footsteps as the man walked along the barrier. A shadow flitted across him and he knew the warrior was just a yard or so away. The Arapaho stopped and coughed.

Fargo placed his right hand on the hilt of the Arkansas toothpick. A quick lunge, a strong thrust, and there would be just the one left to deal with. But as he pulled out the knife the short warrior continued toward the fire.

Supporting himself on one knee, Fargo rose high enough to extend the Sharps. Before he could fix a bead, the short Arapaho veered over to the women. Both saw him coming and sat up, Flora cowering against Kendra.

The warrior swayed with every stride he took. On reaching them, he leaned down and wrapped his fingers in Kendra Hadden's long blond hair. She tried to jerk free and was thrown to the ground. The brave seized her again and headed northward, dragging her up the wash.

Fargo centered his sights and was ready to fire when the warrior unexpectedly stooped and hefted Kendra over a shoulder. She fought but there was little she could do, trussed as she was. Now Fargo no longer had a clear shot, so he angled the barrel to put a slug through the man's knee.

There was a harsh yell and the tall warrior hastened over. They argued, revealing by their gestures that the tall brave insisted that Kendra be left alone and the short Arapaho refused.

Fargo needed a different angle. He scooted ten feet to the left, then rested the rifle barrel on top of the barrier. The Arapahos were so busy snarling at one another that neither noticed him. He took precise aim, leaning forward as he did, forgetting for the moment that the brush forming the barrier was not sturdy enough to bear his weight. He learned the hard way, as the barrier collapsed under him with a crackling of shorn limbs and he pitched onto his elbows.

Glancing up, he saw the two warriors whirl, and as one they charged.

13

Those who intended to survive in the wilderness could not afford to make blunders that put their lives in peril. Skye Fargo rarely did. In this instance, though, his concern for the countess had made him careless, and now he stood to lose more than his pride unless his reflexes were equal to the danger he faced.

Fargo pushed upward and brought the Sharps to bear . . . or tried to, his right arm hampered by being entangled in the brush. He gave a hard jerk and freed himself, only to find a tumbleweed was clinging to his elbow. As he shook his arm to dislodge it, the tall warrior rushed toward him, elevating a tomahawk.

In a fight to the death, split-second decisions meant the difference between living and dying. Fargo did not have a chance to aim, so he fired from the hip, one-handed, the recoil tearing the rifle from his hand.

The bullet hit the tall warrior low on the left side and spun him completely around. He staggered but did not stop, and taking a huge bound, he swung the tomahawk.

Fargo was trying to rise. He threw out both hands and snatched hold of the Arapaho's wrist, preventing the blow from landing. The jolt threw him off balance, and the next moment he was bowled over, landing hard on the barrier with the brave on top of him. Sharp limbs gouged into his back and sides. A branch raked his cheek.

Twisting, Fargo heaved the warrior from him and shoved clear of the brush. He gained his feet first and turned, drawing the Colt, knowing there was nothing that could save the brave now. But he was wrong.

"Skye!" Kendra Hadden screamed. "Behind you!"

Burly bands of rock-hard muscle encircled Fargo from

the rear, and fetid breath that stank of alcohol fanned the side of his face. He felt his boots leave the ground, and he was whirled like a leaf in a chinook and sent crashing to the earth on his shoulder.

Fargo heard Flora screech. The two warriors were in front of him, attacking shoulder to shoulder. They thought to overwhelm him, but they thought wrong. He snapped off four shots so swiftly the blasts sounded like one, and as the echoes rolled up and down the wash the two Arapahos fell face-first to the dirt.

"Skye! Are you hurt?" the countess called out.

A toss of his head was Fargo's answer. He did not take his eyes off the warriors until he verified they were dead. Reloading, he hurried to Kendra. "What about you?" he asked.

She mustered a brave smile. "A little the worse for wear, but nothing I won't recover from." Her features clouded. "Which is more than I can say for Revis and the others. They're all dead. Every last one."

"Not Hollis," Fargo said, sinking to her side. He drew the toothpick and made short shrift of the ropes. As the last one parted, she surprised him by throwing herself into his arms and holding him close.

"Thank you," she said in his ear.

"My pleasure," Fargo said, his lips brushing her neck. That light touch was enough to send an electric ripple through his body. His manhood stirred, twitched. He would have liked to hold her longer, but an anxious voice goaded him to separate.

"Hey! What about me, damn it! Get these ropes off me before those other savages come back!"

Fargo freed Flora and received a taunting grin instead of a hug. Moving rapidly, he picked up the Sharps and the rifle the tall warrior had left by the fire, then hurried to the barrier. Some of the horses, spooked by the gunshots, had fled through the gap, but there were plenty left. He selected two and held them so the women could mount.

"We're forgetting something," Kendra said, gazing at the body of Elizabeth Hadden. "It isn't fitting for us to leave without burying her."

"There's no time," Fargo said.

"Please, Skye. I could never forgive myself if I left her there like that."

"She's right," Flora threw in. "Elizabeth was a raving bitch, but she deserves a decent burial."

Fargo never ceased to be amazed by the attitude of most whites toward death. To his way of thinking, once a person died their body was so much worm food, and it didn't matter at all whether the body was planted six feet under or left to waste away under the sun. But most folks didn't see it that way. To them, a corpse deserved special treatment— sometimes better treatment than the person who had died was given when alive. He was going to outright refuse when Kendra took his hand in hers.

"For my sake."

The hint of promise in her eyes and the way she spoke was all the persuasion Fargo needed. "We can't dig a hole," he answered, "but we can do the next best thing."

Rocks of various sizes dotted the wash. In under ten minutes the three of them had gathered enough to cover Elizabeth from head to toe.

"Someone should say a few words," Flora commented when they were done.

"I'm not a Bible-puncher," Fargo said, taking their arms to steer them to the horses. He didn't believe Eagle Claw would show so soon, but he did not care to linger and be proven wrong. Once the women were on horseback, he had them move off a short distance. Then taking off his hat, he walked to the back of the nook in which the animals were penned.

At Fargo's first whoop the horses that had still been sleeping lurched to their feet. He had to wave and whistle and shout only a few times to incite the thoroughbreds into fleeing, and as they thundered out across the plain he beckoned the women and jogged southward.

"Where to now?" Flora asked.

"To fetch my horse," Fargo said. "We have to get Hollis, then head southeast and hope we can outrun the Arapahos."

"That's twice you've mentioned him," Kendra said. "He went hunting with Ashley this morning. Is Ashley with him now? Where are they?"

Fargo supplied a brief explanation.

"So my husband might be dead," was all Kendra said at the conclusion, not sounding at all brokenhearted by the news.

The Ovaro was right where Fargo had left him. He stepped into the stirrups and rode up out of the wash. "Stay close to me," he advised. "I don't want you wandering off in the dark."

"What are our chances?" Flora asked.

"That depends on how badly Eagle Claw wants you," Fargo responded. "He's already lost a lot of men, so he may decide you're not worth losing any more over. But if he's taken a fancy to either of you, he'll track us all the way to the gates of Fort Leavenworth."

"I won't let them capture me a second time," Kendra vowed.

"Can either of you use a rifle?" Fargo inquired, holding out the one taken from the tall warrior.

They both shook their heads.

"Figures," Fargo said. He paused long enough to load the Sharps and stuff the spare firearm into his bedroll. Flicking the reins, he trotted off, the countess on his right, Flora on his left. For the next hour no one uttered a word. They made good time, even though Fargo stopped to listen at every suspicious sound.

They were crossing a flat expanse, the wind whipping their backs, when Kendra Hadden cleared her throat. "Tell me truthfully, Skye. Is there a fair possibility Ashley is still alive?"

"Afraid so," Fargo said. "He could be waiting with Hollis right this minute."

Kendra bowed her head. "He'll be devastated when he hears about Elizabeth."

"It's partly his own fault," Fargo said. "He had no business dragging all of you out here. The country west of the Mississippi is no place for greenhorns."

"You manage quite well."

Fargo stared at the rippling plain. "I wouldn't be happy anywhere else. This kind of life gets into a man's blood. He can roam wherever he likes, living off the land as he goes, with no strings attached."

"True freedom. I envy you. Some say it's the most precious gift of all."

Flora made a choking sound. "Freedom my foot! The only precious gift I want is a long soak in a hot tub followed by ten hours of blissful sleep in a four-poster bed."

The moon rose ever higher as they rode steadily onward. Fargo reckoned on reaching Hollis before dawn, but the sun had cleared the horizon when the burned-out wagon appeared ahead. He galloped the rest of the way, looking for some sign of the manservant or his horse. Neither was to be seen. But there was evidence that a fire had been built the night before.

"I don't understand," Flora remarked. "Isn't this where you said you left him?"

"Yes."

"Maybe he headed back on his own."

Fargo remembered Hollis's interest in the location of the wagon trail, and shrugged. "Could be," he replied.

At that moment a fluttering groan arose in the grass thirty feet away, riveting the three of them in place. Fargo broke the spell first and lashed the Ovaro toward the sound. He spied a skinny form sprawled down and flew from the saddle to Hollis's side.

The Englishman had been shot in the back, at the base of the spine, and the slug had punched out the front of his stomach. He had to be in tremendous agony.

"Who—?" Hollis asked, blinking as he was gently rolled over. He saw Fargo and said, "Oh, it's you, Yank. I thought it was the bastard who shot me, come back to finish me off."

Kendra and Flora rushed up and knelt, their features registering their shock.

"Good heavens!" Hollis declared, delighted. "You saved them, sir! I can go to my Maker with my soul at peace." He closed his eyes and groaned again, his whole body trembling.

The countess looked at Fargo, who shook his head.

"Abner," Kendra said, tenderly touching the dying man's chin. "Is there anything we can do for you?"

Hollis licked his lips. "Yes," he croaked. "Get him."

"Who? The savage who did this?"

"It wasn't an Indian."

"Then who is to blame?"

The manservant roused and looked at her. "Your husband is the one who laid me low, Countess. Me, the man who waited on his every whim for going on fifteen years.

Me, the man who treated him as if he were my very own son." Tears spilled from Hollis's eyes and he stopped, choking on his emotion.

Kendra stared at the gaping hole where his belly had been. "Ashley did *this*?"

"He showed up late last night on foot. Saw my fire and snuck in close. You should have seen how happy he was to see me, at first." Hollis coughed and had to struggle to go on. "Seems he rode his horse to death escaping from the redskins."

"But why would he shoot you?"

"*My* horse, Countess. He was afraid the savages were still after him and he needed it to get away. I wanted to ride double but he wouldn't hear of it. Told me we'd never make it together. And since his life was worth more than mine . . . " Hollis let the statement trail off.

"Dear God!" Kendra exclaimed.

Flora turned away and cried softly.

"I said he could have the horse and I'd walk," Hollis resumed. "But he didn't want it known that he'd left me to die. You should have seen him, Countess. He was cold as ice, that man. I turned and ran, begging him not to shoot, saying I would never tell anyone." He gasped and winced, holding his stomach. "But he shot me anyway. Shot me and left me lying here rolling around in my own blood. That wasn't the worst, though."

"What could be worse than cowardly murder?" Kendra asked, horrified.

"He rode over, watched me a while, and laughed."

Fargo saw the color drain from Kendra's face. She started to swoon and he caught her and held her until she had recovered and could straighten on her own.

"You think you know someone," Hollis had gone on weakly. "I saw how he was acting on this expedition, how touchy he was at every little thing that went wrong. I thought it was the strain getting to him. Now I'm not so sure." He looked down at himself. "Now I think that I wasted the past fifteen years working for a man whose heart is as dead as those bloody trophies he likes to collect."

"How long ago did he leave?" Fargo asked.

Hollis thought a moment. "An hour and a half, no more." His hand closed on Fargo's leg. "Get him for me, mister. There's no place in this world for demons like him. I—" He stopped, his head snapping back. His body broke into convulsions and he uttered a high-pitched wail.

Kendra put her arm around Hollis to comfort him and stroked his wrinkled brow. He tried to tell her something but the attempt proved too much. He died with her tears watering his cheeks.

This time Fargo did not object to the burial. He dug the shallow grave himself, scooping it out with a charred piece of wood from the wagon. The women helped lower the body. Then Kendra removed her wedding ring and set it on the manservant's chest. Fargo covered the corpse without comment.

Over an hour had been lost. Once mounted, Fargo led them at a gallop to make up for lost time. He knew of a seasonal stream they would reach by nightfall and hoped there would be enough water in it to slake the thirst of their horses. Often he scoured the trail behind them, but the Arapahos did not appear.

Flora rode at Fargo's side. Kendra hung back, deep in thought. When they stopped at midday to give their mounts a breather, she sat by herself and refused to be drawn into conversation.

"I'd be worried about her if I didn't know she's a lot stronger than anyone thinks," Flora confided to Fargo. "She's quite a woman, she is."

"I can see that for myself."

Flora grinned. "Men! American, English, or Swahili, you're all alike. You only have one thing on your minds." She made sure the countess was looking the other way and pinched his thigh. "Not that I would have it any other way." Turning serious, she leaned over and whispered, "Treat her nicely, handsome, or I'll come after you with a carving knife."

Fargo took that as his cue to mount up. They had gone but a short distance when he came on tracks less than two hours old, made by a single horse heading to the southeast.

"The earl?" Flora wondered.

"The earl."

Kendra heard and rode up to see the hoofprints for herself. "If he reaches Kansas City he'll never be made to pay for what he's done. It will be his word against ours, and he can afford the services of the best barristers that money can buy."

"Barristers?" Fargo said.

"Sorry. You call them lawyers."

"We call them a lot worse than that," Fargo said, but neither of the women cracked a smile. He followed the tracks, pacing the Ovaro so their horses would not tire too soon.

This time Kendra did not lag. She rode close to the pinto, so close her stirrup occasionally brushed Fargo's, and after an hour of travel she glanced at him. "I've been thinking. I don't want Ashley's blood on your hands."

"That depends on him."

"He won't let you turn him over to the authorities."

"I'm counting on that."

Kendra reached out to touch his arm. "You can't simply walk up to him and put a bullet in his brain."

"No, I can't," Fargo admitted. "But knowing your husband, that won't be necessary."

Kendra scrutinized his face. "Why do I have the feeling that you've done a lot of killing in your time?"

Fargo gave a toss of his head to encompass the boundless prairie. "In the West killing is as much a part of life as eating and breathing. A man never knows from one day to the next whether he'll be around to greet the dawn." He paused. "Hostiles, outlaws, wild animals, any one of them can do a man in. He has to be ready to kill or be killed. Sure, I've done my share. But never in cold blood."

"Our lives have been so different. Until I met Ashley, I'd never known a moment of violence in my whole life."

A gust of cool wind fanned the nape of Fargo's neck and he twisted in the saddle to see that a bank of roiling black clouds now lined the western horizon. Before dark a storm would hit them. He turned around, and for a fleeting second he thought something moved at the extreme limits of his vision. Stiffening his legs, he rose higher for a better look, but there was nothing in sight.

"What is it?" Kendra asked.

"I'm seeing things," Fargo joked.

Twenty minutes later they discovered otherwise. At the

top of a knoll Fargo found dozens of hoofprints where a horse had grazed and an impression where a man had sat for quite a while.

"The earl rested here, didn't he?" Flora inquired.

Fargo nodded. "He learned his lesson after riding his other horse to death."

"Did he see us?" Kendra was interested in learning.

Again Fargo nodded, pointing at the line of tracks on the other side. "See those? They're deeper going than they were coming. He saw us, all right, and hightailed it."

The prospect of the earl eluding them made them all somber. Fargo rode faster, wishing he dared leave the women to go on alone. By himself he stood a good chance of being able to chase the nobleman down.

As if she had read his thoughts, Kendra made that very suggestion.

"I can't," Fargo said.

"Don't worry about us. Show us how to use a rifle and we'll be fine."

"Not if the Arapahos show their hides. And not with a storm on the way."

"He has to be stopped."

Fargo saw no sense in arguing, so he just didn't answer.

"Please listen to me," Kendra pleaded. "If we don't stop him, Ashley will be free to kill again some day. He'll go on mistreating people, whipping people." She paused. "And he'll be free to make my life a living hell. His family has tremendous influence, great political clout. I know he'll stop me from getting a divorce."

"She's telling the truth, Skye," Flora interjected.

"I know him," Kendra continued. "I know how his mind works. I'll be made a prisoner in his castle. Kept under guard twenty-four hours a day. I'll never be permitted to go anywhere alone, and my mail will always be censored."

"And I'll be fired," Flora said. "He'll replace me with someone he picks."

"So you see, Skye," Kendra added, "you have to go after him. I'd rather be dead than endure such a nightmare. You're my only hope."

Before Fargo could answer, he saw a peculiar sight ahead and immediately reined up.

Scores of antelope were bounding toward them. Covering the ground in immense, graceful leaps, the pronghorns ran with their mouths open, their eyes wide. They paid no attention at all to Fargo and the women, which was so out of character that Fargo knew they were stampeding in mindless fright. At the last instant, the leaders swerved to go around and the rest flowed in their wake.

"My word!" Flora exclaimed.

"Do they do that often?" Kendra asked.

"Never," Fargo said, turning to watch the white rumps speed westward. As usual a buck was at the very back, serving as rear guard. "It's rare to get this close to them. They can spot a person from four miles off."

"What set them off?" Kendra wondered.

"I don't know," Fargo said, urging the pinto on. He hadn't gone fifty yards when he saw more animals racing toward them, this time a small bunch of white-tailed deer, bucks and does both. The deer scattered, some going right, some left, and reformed once they had sped by, their white tails erect.

"I must say," Kendra remarked, "this prairie of yours is a constant source of surprises."

The next moment a flock of sparrows winged past, chirping wildly.

"What does all this mean?" Flora asked.

Fargo had an idea, but he kept his own counsel. It couldn't be true, he told himself. Only a madman would have done so unthinkable an act. Galloping forward, he saw jackrabbits off to the left, springing westward in frenzied haste.

"Oh, look!" Flora cried, pointing at a raccoon with two young ones. "Aren't they adorable?"

"Where are all these animals headed in such a hurry?" Kendra questioned.

"They're running away," Fargo said.

"From what?"

"That," Fargo responded, pointing at the eastern horizon, which was framed by a long line of gray tendrils snaking skyward.

Kendra squinted., "Is that smoke?"

"It sure is," Fargo said. "The earl has set the prairie on fire."

14

To be caught in a prairie fire was a terrifying ordeal and every bit as deadly as a buffalo stampede. A solid wall of crackling flame, sometimes rearing six feet high, roared across the plain faster than a man could run. The fire engulfed everything in its path, the heat often so intense that animals were fried to death while in flight. And if the flames failed to kill them, the smoke would not.

All true frontiersmen knew the danger. As a result they were careful about their campfires, cigarettes, and pipes. Any man who accidentally started a fire was looked down on as incompetent, and no one wanted him for a partner.

Skye Fargo knew the perils of the prairie fire. But on first spotting the smoke, he grinned, thinking Hadden had outsmarted himself, because the wind was blowing from west to east and would blow the fire right back at him. Then Fargo realized the wind had shifted and was sweeping the flames in his direction, and his grin died.

"How could he do such a thing?" Kendra had cried. "Destroy so much just on the off chance he'll destroy us? I didn't think that even *he* was capable of this!"

"Your husband plays for keeps," Fargo said. The smoke stretched for as far as he could see on either side. They had to outflank it, but he had no idea which way was the safest to go, and if he was wrong they could well end up dead.

"We should head west," Kendra said. "Into the storm. The rain will put the fire out."

"He's counting on us to do just that," Fargo said. "It'll buy him the time he needs to pull so far in front of us that we'll never catch him."

"What else can we do?" Flora asked nervously.

"We go around," Fargo said, angling to the southeast.

More and more small animals were racing past, including rabbits, prairie dogs, and mice. A huge rattler slithered by, causing the two thoroughbreds to shy.

"How did he start so big a fire so rapidly?" wondered Kendra.

"It doesn't take much when the grass is this dry," Fargo replied. "All he had to do was make a torch and ride in a straight line for a quarter of a mile or so. The fire spread quickly once the wind caught it."

In fact, the blaze was now a mile wide and several hundred yards across in places, forming a sizzling band that no living thing could penetrate. The northern half of the fire line was advancing faster and had outdistanced the southern half by two hundred feet.

Fargo galloped hard, searching for a break in the flames. Sometimes there were gaps in the fire line where the fire had jumped a short stretch, and while trying to get through was terribly risky, it was the only way they wouldn't fall hopelessly behind Ashley Hadden.

Presently Fargo saw such a gap, an eight-foot-wide path of untouched grass that wound to the other side . . . or seemed to. Fargo couldn't be certain because of the smoke. Yet he plunged in anyway, since it was now apparent he couldn't reach the end of the fire line before the flames swallowed them up.

A wave of blistering heat struck Fargo with the force of a physical blow. On both sides raged infernos, the noise nearly deafening. Smoke wafted above him. Slim gray fingers drifted in front of his face, causing him to hold his breath for long stretches.

Fargo had to slow down. The path had narrowed to under six feet and was slowly shrinking with each passing yard. He feared he had blundered and boxed them in, and he glanced around to see how the women were doing.

Kendra and Flora rode single file, the countess in the lead. They were keeping up with him, but both were coughing and their mounts were acting up.

Fargo pressed on, pulling his bandanna up over his mouth. A cloud of smoke drifted in front of him, cutting off his view. The fire danced within a few inches of the stallion on both sides and the heat was so bad he thought his buck-skins might burst into flame.

Swatting at the smoke with his hat, Fargo drew rein in alarm on seeing a searing red-and-orange wall ahead. There was no way out! The flames would hem them in and burn them to a cinder. He edged forward a few feet, desperately searching for an opening of any kind, and was overjoyed to find a slim three-foot space between the closing sheets of flame.

"Follow me!" Fargo shouted, using his spurs. The Ovaro jumped at the gap, hurtling through with the fire licking at its legs and sides. They sailed beyond the conflagration, alighting on charred earth.

Instantly Fargo wheeled, watching the spot where he had emerged. Kendra made it in a burst of speed and went a dozen yards before stopping. Seconds elapsed, and Flora had yet to appear. He moved toward the opening to go to her aid when suddenly the flaming sheets joined. There was a terrified whinny, a sharp cry. "Flora!" he yelled.

"Save her!" Kendra said urgently.

Then the flames parted and Flora was in the clear, cling-ing to the back of her mount as she was racked by a cough-ing fit.

Fargo moved to her side and held her horse until she had hacked the smoke from her lungs and could go on.

"I hope I never have to do that again!" she commented.

The prairie fire was rushing westward. Fargo saw a dead ground squirrel nearby, its flesh blackened, its lips drawn back to expose its front teeth.

"Ashley almost had us," Kendra said.

No one disputed the point. Fargo assumed the lead, avoiding patches where flames still burned and areas that gave off a lot of smoke. He had to go half a mile before he came to virgin prairie again, and here he stopped to check the legs of all three horses. The front legs of Flora's mount had been singed, but not badly enough to need treatment.

Shortly before nightfall a ragged line of trees appeared. Fargo indicated them and mentioned the stream.

"I'll drink it dry all by myself," Flora declared.

"Not every last drop," Kendra joked. "Save me a pool big enough for a bath."

A mental picture of the countess stark-naked, droplets glistening on her satiny skin, was enough to give Fargo a thirst of a different order. "Just hope there's any water at all," he remarked. "At this time of year it might be bone-dry."

"Please, no," Flora addressed the heavens.

They were forty yards out when the Ovaro lifted its head and sniffed. Fargo smiled at the ladies, saying, "That's a good sign. There must be water after all." He made for an opening in the trees and halted in an oval clearing that bordered a streambed containing a trickle six inches wide and two inches deep.

"Drat," Flora said. "I was beginning to like her idea of taking a bath."

"It's better than nothing," Fargo said, slipping from the saddle. He took the stallion into the bed and draped the reins over the saddle horn. "Drink up," he coaxed.

The Ovaro looked off instead, staring at a thicket.

Fargo stared at the vegetation, saw no cause for concern, and bent his knee to scoop water into his palm. A metallic click caused him to freeze halfway to the ground. The raspy cackle that followed sent a ripple of apprehension down his spine.

"Well, well, we're having a reunion," Ashley Hadden said as he strode from concealment, his rifle in hand.

Both women gasped. Kendra released her horse and started across the stream, her fists bunched.

"Don't be so impetuous, my lovely wife," the earl warned, swiveling the rifle toward her, stopping her in her tracks. "I can imagine how elated you are to see me again, but you really must restrain your passion."

"Bastard!" Kendra snapped.

Hadden came to the edge of the streambed. "Is that any way for a lady to talk, I ask you?" he mocked her. "Or have you been spending all your time with buckskin-clad gutter-trash of late?"

"You murdered Hollis!" Kendra accused him. "And you nearly did the same to us with that fire you set!"

"How *were* you able to avoid that? I thought I had you there." The earl did not wait for an answer, but focused on Fargo. "It was all your doing, I suspect. I should have had

153

you run off the day you appeared. You've been a thorn in my side ever since." Hadden aimed at Fargo's chest. "Now I would like all three of you to back off a little ways and turn around with your hands in the air. Anyone who refuses will be shot dead without hesitation."

It was nerve-wracking to comply, but Fargo did as he was directed. He kept expecting a slug in the back, but all he heard were footsteps. Then the rifle barrel brutally gouged into his spine and he fell to his knees, his legs tingling madly. A second blow, to the back of the head, left him face down in the dirt. He was stripped of the Colt and the toothpick.

"Now I can breathe easier," Hadden said, throwing the six-shooter and the knife behind him as he backed off. Sitting on the opposite edge, he rested the rifle across his legs and grinned like a cat that had just caught three canaries. "Why don't you ladies have a seat too? We have a few items to discuss."

Fargo marshalled his strength and rolled over, resisting the dizziness that tried to swamp his mind. Kendra was on his right, a study in simmering rage. Flora sat on his left, fright making her lower lip tremble.

"First off, where is Elizabeth?" the earl asked. "I saw that she wasn't with you earlier, and I've been dreading the worst ever since."

"The Arapahos killed her," Fargo said when neither of the women answered.

Genuine sadness bowed Hadden's shoulders. "I'm distraught to hear that. She was the best sort of sister a bloke could have. How exactly was she slain?"

Once more Fargo gave the details.

"So it was quick at least," Hadden said.

"Which is more than can be said about sweet Abner!" Kendra flashed with anger. "He died an agonizing death thanks to you."

"Why are you so upset? Hollis was a nobody, a commoner of no great value to the human race. No one will mourn him, no one cares a whit about his passing—"

"I do!" Kendra said. "I was there when he died, and I buried my wedding ring with him."

"You did what?"

"You heard me. Our marriage is over. As soon as we return to England I will petition for a divorce."

Fargo tensed to shove Kendra to safety should the earl open fire. But to his surprise, the Englishman only laughed.

"*You'll* petition? You pathetic wench! Do you really think I will allow you to make me the laughingstock of Great Britain?" Hadden shook his head. "At one time I toyed with the idea of a divorce and thought it might be in my best interests. That was before I saw another, better means to put an end to this farce we call a marriage."

"What means?"

"I'll simply kill you."

The countess started to rise and Fargo grabbed her wrist. "Don't," he whispered. "Not yet."

"I've already killed that simpleton Abner," Hadden went on. "What's one more?" He patted his rifle. "Actually, I owe Hollis a debt for giving me the idea. It wasn't until after I shot him that I realized a man could kill someone out here and no one would ever be the wiser." He looked up. "You see, I had assumed the Arapahos disposed of you."

"Our deaths will be on your conscience," Kendra said.

"What conscience? My dear, in case you're not aware of it by now, I don't have one." Hadden chuckled.

"You're disgusting."

"Call me all the names you like. It won't change the inevitable. In five minutes I'll be alive and you'll be dead."

Flora fidgeted and said, "How will you explain our deaths to the authorities? There is bound to be an investigation."

"I will insist on one," the earl responded. "I'll want the newspapers to carry the whole story of how most of my dear countrymen were killed in a buffalo stampede, and how those who weren't had the misfortune to be slain by marauding Arapahos." He leaned back. "Think about it. I'll go back to England the martyred hero. I lost my precious wife, my devoted servants. Everyone will be falling all over themselves to be nice to me. Why, I might earn an audience with the king himself."

Kendra rose before Fargo could stop her. "I can't permit that."

"You can't stop me."

For the past minute Fargo had been digging his fingers into the soil without being noticed, filling each hand with dirt. He wanted to lure Hadden closer, and to that end he said, "Turn your back on him, Countess. Like most cowards, he can't stand to meet the eyes of the people he shoots when he pulls the trigger."

The earl leaped off the bank and stalked forward, his rifle trained on Fargo. "Cowardly, am I? I should think I proved different at the wallow."

Fargo sat straighter, his hands at his sides. He stared down the barrel of the rifle and tried to think of a way to distract the nobleman for just a second.

Kendra inadvertently did exactly that by stepping between them and saying, "I won't let you harm him, Ashley. You'll have to kill me first."

The moment the countess moved, Fargo rose into a crouch. He heard the earl swear and saw him grip Kendra's shoulder and roughly push her out of the way. As that happened, he pounced, flinging the dirt and swatting at the rifle. So swiftly did he spring that Hadden was caught flat-footed. Fargo reflected the barrel as the rifle went off, and then he tackled the earl and downed him in the streambed.

Blinking feverishly to clear his eyes, the nobleman lashed out in a stiff-armed blow to the upper chest.

Fargo felt as if he had been shot. A tremendous spasm rocked him and he thought he might pass out. Girding himself, he drove a fist into Hadden's gut, doubling the earl over. In return he was hit on the side of the head and knocked sideways. Woozy, he struggled to rise, wondering why the nobleman didn't finish him off. The answer was right in front of him.

Kendra had jumped on her husband and was flailing furiously at his face. Hadden landed a punch to the jaw that sent her reeling, and in a wild dive he seized hold of the rifle.

A single step and a flying jump and Fargo was on the earl again. The rifle stock streaked past his face. He rammed an elbow into Hadden's side, gripped the rifle, and tore it loose. Hadden's own elbow caught him on the cheek, splitting his skin. He aimed a swing that might have ended the fight, but Hadden ducked under it and used one of those rigid spear-hand blows on his neck.

Stars danced before Fargo's eyes and he tumbled backward, still holding the rifle. The earl lunged, an arm upraised, his face the face of a man who had lost all control. His clawed fingers stabbed at Fargo's eyes. Fargo got both arms up in time, and for a heartbeat they were locked nose to nose, the earl growling like a feral dog.

Unexpectedly Flora was there, kicking at the nobleman's side. Hadden bellowed and lashed out with his right leg, striking her in the shins, sweeping her off her feet. Yelping, she tumbled into the water.

Fargo arched his spine and flipped both of his legs upward, hurling the earl over his head. He scrambled erect and barely got his arms up to protect himself from the human cyclone who waded into him with hands and feet raining blows. Hadden resorted to the same flashy kicks and hand strikes he had employed at the wallow, but this time Fargo knew what to expect and was better able to counter them.

They traded hits, splashing through the stream. Fargo knew both of his boots were wet, but he did not think much of it until he stepped on a large flat stone seconds later and his left foot slid out from under him.

Like a bird of prey, Hadden swooped in, his right hand slashing.

It felt as if a war club had slammed into Fargo's side. He couldn't breathe and his ears rang. He doubled over, felt a foot low down on his spine, and was thrown onto his back. His head was yanked up to expose his neck for the kill.

The earl had won. One cutting stroke of his hand and Fargo would die. But instead of seizing the moment, he paused to gloat. "Now you're mine, you son of a bitch!"

That brief delay was all Fargo needed to coil his right leg and spear his boot into the Englishman's gut. The earl tottered rearward, recovered, and spotted the Arkansas toothpick lying close by. Smirking, Hadden dived and came up holding the glittering blade.

Fargo had seen something, too. He'd spied the Colt, and as the earl went for the knife he went for the six-shooter, leveling it as the nobleman sprang. His first shot stopped

Hadden cold, twisting him to one side. His second shot ripped through Hadden's shoulder as the earl drew back the blade to throw it. His third and fourth shots lifted Ashley Hadden off his feet and dumped him in the water.

In the quiet after the gunshots the only sounds were those of three people breathing heavily. Fargo slowly stood, stepped to the body, and dragged the Earl of Somerset out of the stream. He turned to the women. "Either of you hurt badly?"

Flora shook her head while rubbing her right shin.

Kendra rose. A dark bruise was taking shape where she had been struck. "I'm fine," she said softly, her troubled eyes on her husband.

"There was no other way," Fargo tried to assure her.

"I know that," Kendra said. "It's just—" She was unable to finish her sentence. Whirling, she dashed upstream, weaving through the underbrush.

"You should go after her," Flora suggested.

"Maybe now is not the time."

"Trust me, Skye. There will never be a better time." Flora waved him off. "Go on, dunderhead! Don't worry about me. I'll be fine."

Fargo nodded and ran. The countess was far-off already, apparently not about to stop before she reached Canada. "Kendra!" he called, but she gave no sign of slowing. He pushed himself, taking shortcuts through thickets and over logs. Even so, he probably would not have caught her so soon if she had not stopped beside a small pool and dropped to her knees, putting her hands over her face.

Halting a few yards away, Fargo said, "You shouldn't go off by yourself. This is grizzly country, and there might be hostiles around."

The countess made no reply, so Fargo stepped closer. He felt awkward disturbing her, but it was for her own good. "Kendra?" he said. She was quietly crying, her shoulders shaking. "We should go back."

"Not yet," Kendra said, the words muffled by her hands. Shifting, she lowered her arms, revealing the smile she wore. She was shedding tears of happiness, not tears of sorrow. "You did it. At long last my nightmare is over."

"I did what I had to."

"It's almost too wonderful to be believed. I thought Ashley was invincible," Kendra said. She touched her cheek and stared at the teardrop on the tip of her finger. "Isn't this awful of me? My husband is dead and I'm so happy I can't stand it!"

Fargo put a hand on her shoulder. "No one can hold it against you, not after all you've been through."

Kendra took his hand in hers. "I want to thank you." She pressed her full lips to his palm and flicked her tongue across his skin. "Thank you properly." Her tongue roamed to his wrist, then she looked up, the pleading in her eyes as plain as the sudden flaring of lust on her face.

"Here? Now?" Fargo said.

"Why not?"

Under any other circumstances, Fargo would have jumped at the chance. But Flora was all alone, and the Arapahos might show at any time. "We're not out of the woods yet," Fargo said. "And we still have a long ride ahead of us."

The countess stood. Without ceremony she pressed her ripe figure flush against him. Lips so exquisitely soft they melted onto his made him tingle from head to toe. It was the sort of kiss that left a man grateful he was a man, and when it was over, Fargo's manhood was threatening to burst his pants.

"Surely we have a few minutes to spare?" Kendra asked.

"Odds are the Arapahos are hours behind us," Fargo said. "But still—"

Again the countess tried to mold herself to Fargo's body. For someone who did not have much experience, she knew just what to do to drive Fargo over the brink of self-control. She had this curious way of sucking on his mouth that drove him wild. "Please," she said when they broke apart. "I've wanted you from the moment I set eyes on you."

"Flora does have the rifles," Fargo said, weakening. He stiffened when he felt her hand gently close on his organ and stroke it from bottom to top.

"My word. You're so huge."

What little will Fargo had left evaporated. He cupped her bottom and drew her to him to taste her sweet lips once more. Even after all they had been through, she smelled of perfume and powder and other tantalizing scents. Her dainty tongue, so tender, so delicate, teased his mercilessly.

Fargo was no stranger to the physical hunger that sets a man's pulse to racing, but few times had he felt it so keenly. He could not get enough of Kendra Hadden. His mouth covered every square inch of her face, her throat. He glided his hands up and down her back and around front to her quivering belly.

For her part, the countess tried to eat Fargo alive. He knew she had long been starved for affection, knew she was making up for lost time by nibbling or kissing every part of him she could reach. All the while her hand dreamily rubbed his pole.

Fargo placed a hand at the apex of her thighs and rubbed. She gave a low whine as she bit his shoulder. Working a finger between her legs, he stroked the outside of her slit, causing her to stand on her toes and bend her head back, her eyes fluttering.

"Ohhh, Skye! Words can't describe . . . "

Smothering her lips with his, Fargo fondled her womanhood until Kendra panted and wriggled and buried her nails in his back. He kept on caressing her and she tore at his pants, trying to rip them off.

"Not so fast," Fargo said. After waiting so long to have her, he was going to take his time. He pried her fingers loose and she wrapped her arms around his neck.

"It's been so long," Kendra said sadly. "So very damn long."

"A little bit longer won't matter," Fargo responded, closing his fingers over her left breast."

"I can't stand the suspense."

Fargo covered her other breast and massaged both, feeling her nipples harden under her dress. His mouth on hers, he began unfastening her buttons and snaps. The garment was foreign-made, different from most, and it took him a while to figure out a lace eyelet at the throat. When the garment finally folded around her ankles and she stood in the twilight in all her ravishing beauty, a lump came into his throat and his mouth went dry.

"Do you find me attractive?" Kendra asked timidly.

"Do bears like honey?"

Fargo stripped off his hat and shirt, then embraced her. Her skin was hot, her breath scorching. One by one he removed her underthings, gradually arousing her by tweaking her swelling globes and running a finger across her womanhood now and again. She thrilled to his touch, cooing and moaning and panting in his ear.

When Kendra was naked, Fargo surprised her by kneeling, placing his hands on her buttocks, and pulling her toward his open mouth. "What?" she said. His mouth found her core and she tossed back her head, crying, "Oh, God!"

Fargo had to hold her to keep her from slumping to the ground. He lowered her carefully, and when she was on her back he licked and probed, feeling her buck and grind to heighten her pleasure. Her legs closed on his head, clamping him in place.

Around them the trees grew dark but Fargo hardly noticed. While his mouth attended to her pulsing knob, his hands attended to her breasts. He yearned to enter her but held off, waiting for a sign that she was more than ready. It came when she grasped his head and pleaded in a tiny voice.

"I want you inside me! Please, Skye. Now."

Now it was. Fargo positioned himself and dropped his pants. She couldn't take her eyes off his pole as he touched it to her crack. With a smooth roll of his hips he penetrated to her depths. Kendra clasped him close, her nipples digging into his chest, her pelvis pumping of its own accord.

Rocking on his knees, Fargo settled into a steady rhythm. His hands explored her silken skin, his mouth her neck and breasts. She was all he had dreamed she would be, like liquid fire that ebbed and flowed according to his every whim. She was vibrant, pulsing with life and lust and craving the release soon to come.

In the distance a horse nickered, but Fargo did not pay much attention. He was swept up in a bliss so intoxicating he felt drunk, so potent his every pore tingled. A tightening in his loins forewarned him of the impending blast, and he erected a wall in his mind to hold it back until she exploded.

To help Kendra along, Fargo slid a hand between them, down to her throbbing hole. He flicked his finger at just the right spot and Kendra went crazy, scratching and heaving, her teeth buried in his arm. Her slick inner walls rippled in small earthquakes. On feeling her gush, Fargo let himself do the same.

"Ahhhhhhh!"

Time hung suspended as the two of them crested on that plateau where nothing exists except pleasure so pure it is worth its weight in gold. Fargo shook with his release, pounding home again and again. Once over the brink he coasted to a stop and lay quietly on top of her, the breeze cooling their damp bodies.

"That was glorious," Kendra murmured.

"The second helping will be better," Fargo grinned, and raised his head to kiss her. The same horse nickered again. It was the Ovaro, and something was wrong. He pushed off the countess, whispering, "Get dressed. Quickly."

"Why?" she asked sleepily.

"Trouble."

Fargo scoured the trees, wanting to kick himself for letting his desire addle his brain. Donning his shirt, he left it hanging out and buckled his gun belt on over it. A check of the Colt showed he had neglected to reload after shooting the earl. "Damn!" he said, angry at himself as he jammed the new cartridges into the chambers.

"What's wrong?" Kendra inquired. She was putting on her clothes as swiftly as she could, but there were so many she was still on her underthings.

"I don't know yet," Fargo said, moving to the nearest tree so he could study the strip of vegetation to the south. He was startled to see a flickering pinpoint of light through the trees. Someone had built a fire, and he didn't think Flora had the know how.

Kendra took forever, it seemed. At last she joined him, smoothing her dress. "I'm ready."

Taking her hand and holding his pistol in the other, Fargo crept along the stream bed, setting each foot down lightly so as not to make any noise. Kendra imitated him as best she could. They had gone a dozen yards when low voices confirmed Fargo's guess.

"Those are Indians!" Kendra said, aghast.

"Quiet," Fargo directed. He heard gruff laughter and a fearful squeal.

"They have Flora!"

Fargo glanced around. "They'll have us too if you make any more noise."

"Sorry."

Slinking into the brush, Fargo picked his way along until he could see the fire and those around it. Flora Livingstone was in the grip of a husky Arapaho, who appeared to be fascinated by her deep-red hair. Another warrior was carving up Ashley Hadden. The earl's scalp had been removed, and now the brave was removing the nose and ears and other choice body parts. Standing by the horses was a third man, and Eagle Claw held a torch and was reading the sign in the soft earth bordering the water.

"We have to get her out of there," Kendra whispered in Fargo's ear.

"We will. But I can't go rushing in or they might kill her for the sheer hell of it."

"Can't you shoot them?"

"I'd get two, maybe, before the rest reached cover. And the first thing they would do is shoot her."

The countess frowned. "Just when I thought we were finally safe."

"Haven't you learned yet? You won't be safe until you're in Kansas City." Fargo released her and motioned for her to stay still. "Not a peep out of you."

"Be careful."

Fargo sank onto his belly and slunk forward. The warriors were having a fine time talking and chuckling, making so much noise they couldn't possibly hear him. But he was not one to take anything for granted. Ten yards from the fire he had to stop. It was as close as he could go without being seen.

The Arapaho holding Flora was running his fingers through her long hair. She would slap him after each caress, but all he did was laugh and do it again.

"Stop manhandling me, you great bloody brute!"

Having immense fun, the warrior gripped her chin and gave her a vigorous shake.

Fargo saw that Eagle Claw held his Sharps and had the

toothpick tucked under a thin leather belt. Two of the others were armed with rifles. Only the warrior making Flora's life miserable had a lance instead.

All the horses had been tied to a tree. The Ovaro tried diligently to pull loose but was prevented from doing so by the third brave.

Raucous laughter rang out. The warrior working on the earl had taken the nobleman's nose and placed it on his own. His fellows thought he was hilarious.

Fargo was most interested in Eagle Claw. The tall brave had moved close to the spot where Kendra had run off and was bent low to the ground. Once Eagle Claw realized which direction she had gone, the Arapahos would be on her trail like bloodhounds.

A ringing slap turned all eyes toward Flora. The warrior had tried to slip a hand under her skirts and been roundly rebuffed. Annoyed, the brave flung her down and kicked her. She tried to scoot aside and was grabbed by the hair.

"Let go of me, damn your bones!"

"You heard her! Do as she says!"

The Arapahos were not the only ones who swung toward the speaker in amazement. Skye Fargo looked and almost cursed aloud. Kendra Hadden stood on the west side of the stream, shaking her fist as she might at misbehaving children. The brave wearing her husband's nose bolted to her side and seized her arm to pull her to the fire.

"Unhand me this instant!" Kendra snapped in her most imperious tone, and was thrown down the bank. She picked herself up with dignity, then marched over to Flora.

Bewildered, the Arapahos glanced at one another. Eagle Claw spoke and the others scanned the trees and the prairie. Clearly he was suspicious of a trick. He moved toward the women with the torch held high.

Fargo was as puzzled by Kendra's actions as the Indians were, until he saw her glance at his place of concealment. Then he understood and he smiled. She had put her life in danger in order to give him the edge he would need to slay all four warriors before they could reach cover.

The Arapahos were slowly converging, except for the one guarding the horses, who had his cocked rifle wedged to his shoulder. Eagle Claw halted and said something to the man with the lance. The latter pushed Flora from him and hefted the weapon.

The moment was at hand. Fargo crouched, took a running leap, and hurtled into the open doing a rolling dive. A rifle boomed but missed. Surging upright, firing as he rose, Fargo shot the horse-guard in the forehead and swiveled to bang off a shot into the brave about to hurl the lance.

Spinning, Fargo fanned the Colt twice. The slugs thudded into the warrior who had grabbed Kendra, laying him low. There was only one brave, left, Eagle Claw himself, and Fargo pivoted, thumbing back the hammer. He had moved like lightning, but it wasn't fast enough.

Eagle Claw had the Sharps leveled and cocked and was squeezing the trigger when he was slammed into from behind. The jarred rifle fired into the ground. Behind him Kendra beamed and shouted, "Now!"

Fargo couldn't fire. The two women were directly behind the Arapaho. If a bullet went clean through, they'd be hit. He'd started to take a pace to the right so he could shoot without fear of an accident when Eagle Claw barreled into him, catching him around the middle and smashing him to the ground. The warrior jumped astride his chest and whipped the Arkansas toothpick on high.

Fargo's right arm was pinned under Eagle Claw's leg but he could move his gun hand. Without thinking he tilted the barrel at the warrior's groin and stroked the trigger. Eagle Claw jerked at the impact, tensed, and stabbed. Fargo twisted to the right and felt the Arapaho's hand brush against his shoulder. He also felt Eagle Claw's stomach press against the Colt. Immediately he squeezed off his last shot.

Eagle Claw rose once more, face aglow with hatred. He snapped the knife up, then paused. All of a sudden his muscles turned to mush and he slid to one side, dead.

Standing, Fargo remembered his earlier oversight and began reloading. "Are you ladies okay?" he asked.

"I will be, once you get me back to civilization," Flora said. She gave him a sly wink. "Of course, there's no need to hurry on my account."

"I'm fine," Kendra responded, her luscious mouth puckering in a silent kiss. "And I echo her sentiments."

Skye Fargo looked from one to the other and grinned. The rest of the journey promised to be one he'd never forget.

LOOKING FORWARD!
The following is the opening
section from the next novel in the exciting
Trailsman series from Signet:

THE TRAILSMAN #153
SAGUARO SHOWDOWN

*1860, the hot, dry land the army
still called the Department of Arizona,
where the ambitious seized the time
and the place to kill and conquer . . .*

The big man's lake-blue eyes were intent as he watched the scene unfold below and used the widespread, unruly branches of the paloverde as a hiding place for himself and the magnificent Ovaro. This was the third day he watched, intrigued by what he saw. As on the other two days, the young woman rode a cinder-gray quarter horse from the distant ranch, coming to a halt almost at the foot of the hill below him. She ran a hand through full black hair worn loose, and her slender form was clothed in a white shirt and blue Levi's. She dismounted and waved a hand to the short, paunchy figure of a gray-haired man some hundred yards away. Then, with another wave, she leaped into the saddle and sent the horse into an instant gallop.

Bending low in the saddle, she raced the distance to where the man waited, holding a large pocket watch on a silver chain. He consulted the watch as she skidded the horse to a halt and held it up for her to see. They spoke for a moment, then she walked the horse back to the starting point where she repeated the dash again. She made two more runs, the man timing her at each, and when she finished they walked to where a wall of sun-dried clay stood all by itself, attached to absolutely nothing. It had plainly been erected for a single purpose, and Skye Fargo watched from beneath the paloverde branches as the scene below unfolded exactly as he had witnessed it the previous two days.

Four men came from the ranch buildings to join the young woman at the lone wall, which Fargo estimated to be some ten feet in height. They brought grappling hooks which they tossed to catch hold at the top of the wall, pulled themselves up, and lowered themselves down the other side. This time the young woman used the watch. She had them repeat the maneuver over and over until she did the same with another four men who came from the ranch. When the second group finally finished, she took one of the grappling hooks and scaled the wall herself. Even from his distant vantage point, Fargo saw that she was faster than any of the men. She scaled the wall five times and then took the eight men back to the ranch buildings, where they engaged in what was plainly a rehearsal for an attack. Breaking into units of two, or acting individually, they dashed around the corners of ranch buildings, stables, bunkhouses, toolsheds, and the main house, flattened themselves against outer walls, sometimes crawled, and ducked around corners with guns in hand.

When they finally halted the mock attack at a command from the young woman, the day had slid into late afternoon. Fargo's eyes were narrowed in thought. There was little doubt that he had been witnessing training and rehearsal for some kind of attack, and Fargo let his lips purse as the question hung in his mind. Had he run into a stroke of luck? Had he stumbled upon what he had come to find? Perhaps only a part of it, he mused. But he had to be sure. Everything was different in this dry, hot, hardscrabble land. It offered nothing in friendship—everything defensive, bristling, and harsh. He had to be sure before he moved further, and he watched the dusk begin to slide its way across the spare terrain. The weather-scoured basalt rock took on a lavender hue, and the carpet of brittlebush became blue-gray.

He realized that what happened next was his own fault, a lapse of caution. He'd let the first rule of survival—always be alert—slip. As he moved the Ovaro out of the safety of the paloverde, his thoughts had turned to the long and twisting path that had brought him to this southwest corner of Arizona. The four riders spotted him instantly from a little farther up the slope. They came at him at once, spreading out to cut off his flight. Fargo's hand went to the Colt at his side, but he saw the four rifles aimed at him. He could bring down two, maybe three, in a shoot-out, but one was certain to blast him. Besides, he didn't want to risk a shoot-out because it could mean the end of his assignment. It had become personal to him. And he wanted to learn more about the young woman and the strange series of training maneuvers.

He moved the pinto toward the four men, but kept the horse to the outside of the riders. He stayed at a walk until he drew closer to the four men, then in one motion he dug his heels into the ribs of the Ovaro and dropped his body down behind the right side of the horse. He was clinging with but one hand on the saddle horn and one foot in the stirrups as the Ovaro shot forward at a gallop. He heard the two rifle shots go high over the horse and then the shouts of the men as they wheeled to give chase. Pulling himself up into the saddle again, he swerved the pinto into a narrow rock-lined passageway he had explored earlier. He raced the horse halfway through the curving passage, pulled himself up to stand in the saddle for an instant, and leaped onto a flat ledge of rock as the Ovaro raced on. The four pursuers appeared in moments and Fargo, lying flat on the ledge, let the first three pass. The fourth rider, a dozen feet behind the other three, rode past the ledge and Fargo dived as a cougar leaps on its prey.

The man fell sideways from his horse as Fargo landed on

him and hit the ground with all of Fargo's muscled weight atop him. Fargo grimaced as he heard the terrible sound of the man's neck snapping as he landed on a protruding piece of rock. Pushing to his feet, Fargo drew his Colt as he heard the sound of a horse racing back down the passageway. The third rider had found a spot wide enough to turn his horse and charge back again. The rider came into sight, then tried to rein back on his horse as he saw the figure in front of him, the Colt raised to fire. He was too late. The Colt barked and the man clutched at his chest as he toppled from his horse. Fargo dropped to one knee and waited, ready to fire again, as he listened to the sound of hoofbeats coming down the passage.

They drew closer and his finger rested on the trigger. Then the hoofbeats suddenly stopped. The rider had reined to a halt just beyond sight, up the curving passageway. Even on foot, there was no way he could get by without stepping into the line of fire, Fargo knew, and he waited, his every muscle tensed. But the man still didn't appear. He had decided to let his quarry come to him, Fargo realized as he began to back down the passage. A dozen feet further, he turned and began to half-run and half-slide down the smooth rock of the passageway, keeping his ears tuned to the sound of a horse coming after him. He was nearly at the bottom of the pass when he heard the sound of the horse. He shot a quick glance at the walls, saw only sheer, dense rock, and began to run faster in order to reach the base of the passageway first and find a spot to take cover as he fired.

He had almost reached the bottom when he skidded to a halt as he saw a man waiting, his rifle to his shoulder and trained on him. Automatically, Fargo turned and started to run back up the passage when the rider came into sight, rifle raised to fire. Fargo halted, glanced back at the man at the bottom of the passage, and cursed. He was trapped. He'd be cut down by one or the other. Slowly, he lowered the hand holding the Colt and waited as the men moved toward him from both sides. He'd been trapped by men who knew the terrain better than he did. The one at the bottom had come back down through another cut in the rocks and waited while the other had held his attention long enough in the passage, Fargo realized bitterly.

"Drop the gun, you son of a bitch," the man walking toward him from the bottom ordered, and Fargo let the Colt slide from his fingers. "Get back from it," the man said, and again Fargo obeyed as the man came up to retrieve the Colt and push it into his belt. Fargo took in a medium-height figure, thick-set, with a heavy, coarse face and thick lips that protruded froglike. "Call your horse," the man said, and Fargo gave the special whistle the Ovaro would know. In moments, the pinto came down the passageway to halt before him. "Hit the saddle. No tricks or you're a dead man," the frog-lipped one rasped.

Fargo climbed onto the horse and both men came up behind him. At the bottom of the hill the heavy-faced man swung onto his own horse. "Ride straight downhill," he said, and Fargo kept the Ovaro at a walk as he rode to the flat land and toward the distant ranch. As he neared it, he saw that the spread was more substantial than it appeared from a distance—and certainly more opulent, the main house imposingly fashioned of stone and heavy timbers, long and flat-roofed with large windows on each side of a solid front door. The other buildings were all in good repair, he noted, freshly painted, clean, even the toolsheds in good shape. The two men brought him to the door of the main house and came to a halt. "Get down," the heavy-faced one said, and as Fargo swung from the Ovaro he saw the young woman step from the house.

She was really quite striking, he saw at once. High cheekbones gave strength to a face that otherwise might have been simply attractive, with a straight nose, doe-brown eyes, a wide mouth, and full lips. Her body, slender yet full of soft gracefulness, moved with easy confidence, breasts modest but nicely placed, he saw, legs long under the Levi's. "Caught him watching us," the thick-lipped man said.

The young woman's doe-brown eyes moved slowly over the big man in front of her, lingering on the chiseled strength of his face. "Spies are apparently growing handsomer these days," she commented. "Who sent you, big man?"

"Nobody sent me. I was just passing through," Fargo answered.

"Shit you were," the heavy-faced man said, and thrust the rifle barrel hard into Fargo's back.

Fargo kept his eyes on the young woman. "I stopped to watch. I was curious," he said.

"A very convenient answer," she said, and he noticed she had a very direct manner of peering at him from under her black eyebrows. "What's your name?" she asked.

"Fargo . . . Skye Fargo," he said.

Her deep eyes stayed on him. "You're not from around here," she said.

"How do you know?" he tossed back.

"Something about you, something different," she said. "What are you doing here?"

"I told you, passing through. Riding by."

"To where?" she pressed.

"No place special in mind," Fargo said.

"He's lyin'," the heavy-faced man cut in.

"I suspect so too," the young woman agreed, her eyes meeting Fargo's bland gaze. "Lock him up, Ed. Maybe he'll decide to talk after a few days locked up."

"He killed Johnson and Rodrigo trying to get away," the man called Ed put in.

"They were going to kill me," Fargo said.

The young woman frowned as she thought for a moment. "No food or water. That definitely ought to loosen his tongue in a few days," she said. She met Fargo's eyes and her face held a kind of reluctance, along with determination. "It's your choice, big man. You can talk now," she said.

"Nothing to talk about." Fargo shrugged, and saw her lips tighten unhappily as she turned and went into the house. The rifle barrel prodded into his back again, and he was marched forward toward a small square structure, located behind the house and at the edge of a corral. While Ed kept the rifle pushed into his back, Fargo watched the other man unlock the door of the structure, then he was pushed inside. Fargo got a glimpse of a single barren area that had probably once been a storage shed. A small high window let in what little light there was left in the day. Ed slammed the door shut and the room became almost black, as Fargo heard the padlock closing on the other side of the door. He immediately pressed one ear to the door and listened to the voices, which were faint yet clear enough to hear. Ed's voice came first.

"Don't go near him unless I'm here," the man ordered.

"What if he has to go. There's no place in there," the other man said.

"Fuck him," Ed growled.

"She won't like that. She'll say we should've taken him to the outhouse. You know the way she is," the other man said.

"Yeah, I know," Ed muttered. "All right. If he calls, you take him to the outhouse by the barracks—but be careful with him!"

"Don't worry," the other said. "But you know if he stays mum she'll have us keep him until it's over. She won't go for having him killed unless she can be sure about him."

"It won't matter," Ed said. "It'll be too bad about him."

"Too bad about what?"

"About his trying to escape and our having to shoot him," Ed said and laughed. "I figure that'll happen tomorrow night." He laughed again, and Fargo listened to the sound of his footsteps hurrying away. The man had no problem disobeying orders. He had his own plan and he'd carry it out, that was certain. Fargo's mouth drew into a thin line. He was left with no choice now. He hadn't the luxury of waiting for another visit from the young woman, and he sank to the floor as night came to plunge the little structure into pitch-blackness. When the moon finally rose high enough to send a pale light through the small window, he pushed to his feet and went to the door.

He called out as he pounded on the door. "You out there. I've got to go. Let me out," he shouted.

There was silence for a moment and then the voice answered. "Get back from the door," it said, and Fargo stepped back and heard the padlock being opened. "Come on out," the guard called, and Fargo pushed the door open and stepped outside to see the guard holding his rifle aimed at him. "That way," the man said and gestured to the barracks. Fargo saw the outhouse at the far end of the building. The guard stayed back and away from him as he walked forward, but his rifle was aimed and ready to fire. Fargo reached the outhouse and pulled the door open. "Holler afore you come out," the man ordered.

Fargo nodded, stepped into the outhouse, and closed the door after him. Instantly, he reached down and drew the thin, double-edged throwing knife from the holster on his leg. He held the blade in the palm of his hand, waited a suitable length of time, and then called out. "I'm coming out," he said. He counted on the man being a fraction less tense than when he'd opened the shed door, and that fraction was all he needed. He also knew he'd have just one chance, but he had faith in his marksmanship and the accuracy of the thin blade often referred to as an Arkansas toothpick. He pushed the door half open, enough to see the guard waiting a dozen feet away. His hand came up as he pushed the door farther open, and using all the strength in his arm and shoulder, he threw the knife underhand.

The blade whistled through the darkness as he stepped from the outhouse, his eyes on the guard. The man didn't see the thin blade hurtling at him until it was too late. He tried to twist aside but the knife slammed into the side of his neck, embedding itself to the hilt. He staggered sideways, the rifle falling from his hands. He tried to reach one hand up to pull the blade from his neck, but closed his fingers around the hilt of the weapon just as his strength gave out. He collapsed to the ground, his hand falling from the hilt of the blade, twitched for some thirty seconds, and lay still. Fargo ran in a crouch to the man, pulled the knife free, and wiped the blade clean on the man's shirt. He pulled the man's gun from his holster and saw it was a Remington Rider five-shot double-action piece. It would have to do until he could get his Colt back.

Holstering the gun, he ran in a crouch to the stable, where a hurricane lamp burned dimly to afford some light. He found the Ovaro in a back stall, his saddle and the rest of his gear against the rear wall. In moments he had the horse saddled and ready to go. He led the horse from the stable and had just cleared the doors when he heard the shout and then a shot fired into the air. His eyes flicked to where he had left the guard, and he recognized Ed's thickset body bending over the figure on the ground. The warning shot had already set lamplights on in various ranch buildings, and Fargo pulled himself onto the pinto and set the horse into an instant gallop. He raced across the open land at the front of the ranch, staying low in the saddle, and heard Ed shout and fire off two more shots that were far off the mark. Fargo took a low fence at full speed and raced into the night, turning the horse up the slope of the first hill, cutting to his left, and galloping up another low incline. He turned again, and with the pale moon affording enough light, rode into the harsh basalt rock formations to a deep cavern he had found two days earlier.

He entered the cavern, slid from the horse, and retreated deeper into its blackness. It was unlikely they'd try to give chase in the night, but if they did they'd never find him, he knew, and drew a deep sigh, loosening the horse's cinch and pulling off the saddle. They'd left the big Henry in its rifle holster on the saddle, he was happy to see, and he drank from his canteen before he spread his blanket and stretched out. He had already made one decision. He'd be visiting the ranch again, but his way this time. It seemed more likely now than before that the handsome young woman was part of what he had come here to find. But he had to know how and why. If his guess was right, she could be the key to finding out more.

He pulled off his clothes and lay back in the near-total darkness of the cavern. He let his thoughts unreel back to the strange convergence of circumstances that had brought him here, hiding in this dark cavern. He found himself reliving each event as it came alive with crystal clarity. . . .